SEPTEMBERS

By the same author

SEPTEMBERS

Christopher Prendergast

SALT

CROMER

PUBLISHED BY SALT

12 Norwich Road, Cromer, Norfolk NR27 0AX United Kingdom

© Christopher Prendergast, 2014

Printed in Great Britain by Clays Ltd, St Ives plc

Typeset in Sabon 10/13

ISBN 978 1 907773 78 5 paperback

1 3 5 7 9 8 6 4 2

For Mum, Dad and Rich

'The Vindications exist . . .'
   –'The Library of Babel', JORGE LUIS BORGES

THIS ISN'T WHAT I expected. White office blocks pass over my head. We plunge into the Queensway tunnel. Strip lights cast a weak sodium glare over the tunnel walls. Annabel has been driving us in silence for the last twenty minutes. I don't want to ask her where we are going. The car emerges into white sky and I sit up a little. I see a domed roof of Portland stone and other familiar buildings. We are in the city centre during rush hour, next to Centenary Square.

About five years ago a fibreglass statue burnt to the ground here. People were walking past as it happened. There was talk that a teen fumbled some matches he was playing with, dropping a small flame onto the resin which quickly set alight. When I was young I often climbed up on that statue and used it as a play area. It was a crowd scene, a march from industry into the city's future. Kids used to sit in the occasional gaps between the marching figures and dangle their legs down the side of the plinth. In the middle of the crowd no-one could see you. I had my first kiss on that statue.

The car slows. I look for the spot where the statue used to be. There's nothing except a lamppost over a black bench.

The sculptor came back to Birmingham about a week after the fire. He picked through the wreckage but there was nothing to restore. He grew up in the city but he hadn't lived here for a number of years. A charge of arson was raised against a sixteen-year-old but was subsequently dropped. Fibreglass, polyester resin, paint – these alone were enough. The sculptor scratched his head and tried to work out what it all meant. He got on a plane and went back to Paris.

Goodbye, Raymond.

One of the figures on the plinth faced backwards, unlike all the others. She held a palette and brush and turned to the past to kiss it goodbye. I was away from the city, living somewhere else, when it burned down. I didn't even notice it was gone when I came back. My friend pointed it out. He told me about the fire, the sculptor and the girl who was kissing goodbye to everything behind her. She was doing it because the motto of the city is *Forward*.

Centenary Square keeps changing. I can see the blank white fencing around a construction site. They've started building a new library next to the REP theatre. When they haul up that fencing and unveil the new building I have the sense it will be as if a tiny wound has healed. A little nick, made in passing, will blend into the city's skin. The fibreglass statue will be a passing accident. I wonder what really happened, who even remembers.

Eventually we join the traffic on Broad Street. I look around the edge of the seat. Annabel lets go of the steering wheel, wipes her face and grabs the wheel again. She's concentrating. She takes the next turn off, weaves down side-streets and takes us out into a housing estate. We pass blocks of medium-rise flats in grim brick tones. She goes up a couple of gears. She doesn't make a sound except for the creaking of the wheel and the clunking of the gear shifts. I wonder if she is driving back to Sheffield. Is this the way? I stop myself from asking.

The statue fire would be referred to in passing by local

journalists. People seemed to shrug. It quickly slipped off local news reports. When you look at it, there was a broad consensus – *This was OK. We'll let it pass.* This leaves a sense of blamelessness. No-one really saw what happened. Nothing really burned and no-one really burned it. Not intentionally anyway. But I feel differently. I have always taken exception to the event.

I think Annabel may be crying. I feel the back of her seat with my hand. The upholstery is dry and cold but it hints at her familiar outline. I hear her sit forward and breathe out. It's an even breath but a forced one. The car creaks and moans. She's had it for years now. I'm surprised it's still roadworthy. It was her first car, a present from her mom and dad. I bring my hand back and place it on my chest. I don't speak.

My other hand is in my pocket. I'm clutching a small plastic bottle which makes a hard outline in my trouser pocket. I feel the grooves of the lid. My fingertips slide down, over the slightly rough texture of the label which has slipped with the bottle's grease. It has been used recently. A little bit of waste, a little excess went over someone's hands and onto the bottle itself. It wasn't all applied as intended. It's not my lube but the bottle has a perfect, rounded form. I keep turning it around.

At some point Annabel joins the motorway.

'It's not worth it,' she says. 'I don't think I can do it again.'

Her voice is wavering.

'It's your choice' I say. My voice is in the footwell.

'I can't do it.'

Her nails clack on the wheel.

'Why don't *you* ever choose?' she says, angry.

I have never intentionally hurt anyone in my life. I have

fumbled the matches once or twice though. I sit up as she indicates. She slows down. I untangle myself from the limp seatbelt. I move to the middle of the seat but she won't turn around. I can see her wet cheeks. She pulls onto the hard shoulder. A thicket of bare trees lean over the grey boundary. Streaks of oil mark the roadside. She unlocks the door, takes off her seat belt and clatters out of the car all at once. She walks towards the end of the layby.

She thinks about hopping the barrier but the bracken looks too thick. Instead she walks on with her back to the car, towards the point where the layby tapers into the motorway's outside lane. She walks towards this point as if it is a place. As if it has public squares and its own vernacular. As if there are councillors and St Patrick's Day parades. I watch her getting closer and I can hear horns.

JUST DIRECTIONS

I

TWO YEARS AGO, in September, Annabel asked me to
move in. She quickly hid her mouth with a cup of coffee.

'You want me to move in now?' I asked.

'Yes,' she said. 'Don't worry. It's OK if you don't want to.'

'Is it?'

It was Saturday and we were in her flat. We were almost
elbow to elbow around her kitchen table and a slab of sunshine shone from the small window, over our heads, missing
both of us and falling on the chequered pattern of the lino. She
looked over her mug at me and asked when we were leaving.
She moved the whole thing on as swiftly as that. The sunshine
ran over our heads and if we breached it, either of us, there was
a chance we'd be vaporised. She knew that. She was testing to
see if I'd stand up first.

We sat still for a few seconds. Then she said we should
leave. That afternoon, early in autumn, I was happy to think
of Annabel's Peugeot 206 bleeding across a weathered old
map. Her red line was set to move South, down the M1. She
went to stand up and I grabbed her pale arm and told her, with
hushed desperation, to wait. I eyed the slab of light above us.

'Don't cross the light,' I said. 'Don't cross it.'

She breathed heavily and waited for something, her chest moving slow and steady in the white vest. This is how I like to re-

member Annabel, bent towards me, a little naive and waiting, looking for something imperceptible in the light and wielding an impressive cleavage.

It did not take long for me to get the essentials, although it involved us crossing the city centre to my place. I threw my stuff into a black holdall. When I came into the living room Annabel's legs were stretched out across the sofa and she was watching God TV. I don't know which of the four horsemen were forecast to arrive but she looked up at me over a pair of sunglasses and said, 'We better go.'

On the motorway we passed two or three retail parks. The steel skeleton of a distribution centre dominated the skyline for a few seconds then disappeared behind a low hill. After an hour or two we stopped at some services near Leicester to pick up a paper and enough drink for a stash at the hotel. We queued up with the bottles clinking in our basket. Whilst we stood waiting, an argument brewed behind us. A young girl, about sixteen or seventeen and heavily bronzed, started to raise her voice at her clearly older boyfriend. Apparently, he had once referred to her as 'hard work' to his friends.

Annabel was smiling at me. She began playing with one of the twenty or so bracelets that decorated her arm.

'Tell me you're not going to be boring this weekend. Try not to talk about work.'

We moved along. The checkout worker directed me to enter my card into the machine. She sighed and asked me to enter my pin.

'Even if we pass something with a Grade II listing,' Annabel continued, 'try not to go on about it.'

I shook my head and grinned back at her. The couple behind us went silent. They were each standing with their arms folded. We left the building through an amusement arcade. As Annabel checked the map with her feet sticking out of the driver's side, I stretched my legs in the scarcely inhabited car park.

September sunshine lit the concrete to a stunning level. It was as reflective as snow and I tried to shield my eyes as two people approached one of the few other cars. It was the bronze girl who had been standing behind us. She was arguing with the guy again. I watched them both get in the car. At that point the boyfriend – I assumed he was her boyfriend – made a sudden movement so his elbow flashed into view. I could hear him shouting now. I walked over to the car and as I came up to the half-raised window I saw she was cradling her face in her hands. One solitary line of blood was trickling out of her nostril, red as paint. I asked the only thing I could think to say.

'Are you OK?'

The man leaned forward and interrupted.

'We're fine, mate.' He leaned back so I could see her nod pathetically. Then he looked up at me with grey eyes and clenched his teeth. Three lines were cut into his head and one of them ran on through his eyebrow. I couldn't tell which were scars and which were accessories.

'If I were you I'd walk away and go back to your missus,' he said.

I looked at her once again. She was cradling her nose. She tried to rest her elbow on the opposite window. There was more embarrassment in her nervy shaking than anything else. It was like I was her dad. I may as well have caught them copping off in her bedroom. She sighed impatiently.

'You're blocking my sunlight, mate,' he said.

I walked back across the few empty spaces, crossed the painted yellow lines and got back in the Peugeot. Annabel was humming and thinking out loud.

'Everything all right?' she asked.

'Yes. Fine,' I said.

'What did they want?'

I pulled at the neckline of my T-shirt. Annabel stopped fiddling with the ventilator.

'*Matt*,' she said, 'what did they want?'

'Just directions,' I said.

When we were a good twenty miles down the motorway I turned and grabbed a beer from the backseat. Anna flicked the indicator and, as the car straightened up, she started talking again. Despite her earlier warnings about outlawing shop-talk, she kept teasing me, asking whether I'd *gotten used* to Mrs Yeoman. I knew what she was getting at. Annabel thought our professional differences were based on some latent sexual tension.

'She's got a thing for you, definitely,' Annabel said, with relish.

I took a few sips. The beer was still cool from the service station fridges.

'We'll have to postpone that fantasy for another week,' I said.

When we changed lanes I spilt a few drops on the car seat. I rubbed them into the upholstery. Signs counted down to names, then names changed and the numbers shot up again. Annabel and I talked about some travelling we could do in the summer. She wanted to visit most of Europe. Annabel talked on and on, like she wanted to go everywhere. I couldn't keep up.

In the evening we arrived in High Wycombe. It was strange. There were plenty of willing, low-flying executives around. There were also plenty of angry young men cruising around the antiquated cobbled roads, leaning out of their windows. All of them looked eager for contact with strangers.

I took over directing Annabel to the hotel. I had taken a call on her phone from Corinne and they were running late but wanted to meet us in Lakota. Instead of hooking up with them we went to check in and Annabel cracked open a bottle of wine to make up for lost time.

I answered our room door. It was one of the maids bringing extra towels. There was some shame in the amount of alcohol already piled on the table. Annabel eyed me as the maid crossed between us. She asked about the checkout time.

'It's 11am, but we can give you longer if you need it.' The maid sheepishly went to lay the towels on the table, then, seeing there was no room, turned to Annabel who held her hands out.

'There you go. If you need anything else, dial 9 to go straight through to reception.'

The door shut behind her.

'You can invite *her* out if you want, Matt,' Annabel said.

She poured herself a glass of wine before throwing off her vest top. We were on the second or third floor. Looking out of the window, I saw a maze of extensions to the main building, other roofs and a small courtyard, a smoking area or garden.

'I need a cigarette,' I said.

'I need some fresh air. Could you open the window?'

She unclipped her bra behind me. Annabel wasn't a jealous girl – she had no need to be. She was competitive though, so the presence of another woman in *our* bedroom, albeit our hotel bedroom, was enough for her to mark her territory. She stripped entirely and sorted through her clothes. She strolled in and out of the bathroom. I decided to smoke out of the open window.

We were meeting Corinne and Seb, two of Annabel's friends. They were not from High Wycombe, but they came up from London frequently. They had emailed Annabel the directions. It was not apparent to me why they often came. All I could think was that we weren't far from Legoland. I pulled at the window ledge wondering if it might come away and reattach somewhere else.

I offered Annabel a cigarette. She covered herself up in a towel and stood next to me at the window. I kissed her on the neck. Her phone rang. She answered, listened for a minute and smiled. She threw the phone onto the bed and wrapped an arm around my neck. She said we had to make a move. Corinne wanted to tell us something. That was why we were here.

We sat waiting in Lakota. All the coasters strewn about the bar and tables, some at chest and some at waist height, struck me as little parts of something bigger. I wanted to unite them and allow the big thing to make a case for itself. I spun my coaster around, between my forefinger and the dark wooden table. Annabel suddenly stood up like an agent breaking cover and pointed out her friends. The two of them were busy ordering drinks so she quickly sat back down.

Although they had gone to the same school, Corinne was

not one of Annabel's old school friends. They didn't talk at all for a number of years. Their friendship only got off the ground once they started weekend shifts at the same newsagents. Both warranted attention from an early age. It seemed to me, Corinne must have got addicted to this attention and had to move to the capital. Not to say she would get it there, but in some way London offered to compensate.

Corinne wore a grey jumpsuit with black tights and had a streak of peroxide in her hair. She was cosmopolitan. She turned heads with an overpowering laugh. Being northern in London was perhaps her most appealing trait. It struck me as exotic. That more than the Bermudan blood that ran down her Dad's side of the family.

Some way into her time in the capital, following several volatile and short-lived friendships, Corinne had acquired Seb and he made space to move her in. Seb was well paid, gay and lonely. As friends, they kept each other's backs. Seb was tied up in hedge funds. What I liked about Seb was his general awareness of the circus he was involved in. In fact, I liked them both; they were the only double date I could agree to. They never asked about my salary or tried to suggest alternative careers.

Only once, the first time I met him, and very half-heartedly had Seb ever said, 'You should move down here'. He meant London.

'You look nervous.' I said.

'Can you not see her?'

I looked over at the bar. 'She's ordering a drink.'

Annabel shook her head. They walked over to us and Corinne was holding a Diet Coke.

'Hey, Matt! How are those kids treating you?' Seb asked.

It had only been a few weeks. I told him I was still getting bogged down in the paperwork.

Seb patted my arm reassuringly. He grabbed the peak of his flat-cap and tilted it a little. 'You know I've got a manager now who's twenty-two. This guy got fired out of a cannon through the education system. He's phenomenal.'

I asked whether his boss was Etonian.

'Not even. We don't take wannabe MPs. We take the really smart people, handpicked.'

'Do I get a hello, Matthew?' Corinne asked, smiling.

We hugged and I felt the bump of her stomach press up against me.

'It's been six months. There's too much to talk about. Seb's had too many boyfriends to mention.'

Seb went red at this and, just as I was about to offer my congratulations to her, Corinne got her second wind. She explained she couldn't drink that night and did an Adam West-style *darn it* gesture with her fist. Then she reassured us we were all there to get drunk in her stead. She wanted to have fun vicariously. I didn't think there was enough to go around.

Following Corinne's speech Annabel went at it hard, draining her bottles when I had barely touched my pint. We went to a few different bars. At one point we found ourselves wandering around the Eden shopping centre looking for a bowling alley that was closed. Later I found myself talking to Seb about wrestling in our hotel room. For twenty minutes Annabel had been suggesting baby names. When she came up with 'Kurt' I immediately thought of Kurt Angle, the wrestler.

'You know, I had to break up a fight the other day over Kurt Angle,' I said.

Seb didn't know who Kurt Angle was. He'd never watched wrestling.

'You'd call this a sport?' he said after listening.

'It's an art. It's performance,' I said.

He told me some personal horror stories. His classmates used to bully him. They would ask him trick questions, invite the right sort of response and launch themselves at him. He showed me how they compared wrestling slams and holds, shaking their heads at each other in disagreement, snatching at his raised arms and lifting him up. Day after day he went through this at school.

'Crippler Crossface,' I said.

'What?' Seb asked, looking confused.

'I think that first move was the Crippler Crossface.'

'OK. Maybe it was.' He looked past my shoulder. 'So what were the kids fighting about?'

'Nothing,' I said. 'None of them wanted to be Kurt Angle in the Royal Rumble.'

He shrugged.

I sank back into the headboard and motioned for him to pass me another beer. The night hadn't fully materialised. We knew a baby was on the way but I was none the wiser about how it had come to exist. I was beginning to suspect that Corinne and Seb conceived between them, out of a drunken fumble. It couldn't be true though. If they had consummated the friendship it would have been carefully planned. They would have met every day for two weeks in Starbucks about it. Normal and willing sperm wasn't good enough for her. It had to be coveted.

I watched the two girls as they did impressions of their old manager. After a while, Corinne and Seb decided to go back to their hotel. I watched Anna breathe heavily at the end of the bed. She brushed one of her dress straps off her shoulder indignantly.

'Who's Kurt Angle?' she said. Before I could answer she continued. 'He's not one of your kids, is he?'

'He's an American wrestler.'

'A wrestler?' she huffed, and slunk into the bed. 'Wrestle me . . . for once.'

I stood over her, pulling back her hair, and I went to kiss her just as she pulled away. She had motioned to the bathroom and stretched out two fingers; it was either a peace gesture or she meant 'two seconds'. The room was a bombsite of drink. Seb had left half a bottle of red. Small items of clothing were on the bed. I hadn't noticed her take off some of the bracelets. These things didn't look like ours but I doubted either of our guests would have felt the need to deposit them. I stood by the toilet door. Anna was quiet.

Her shadow moved in the light at the bottom. It moved slowly. Then I realised she was being sick. I tried the door but it was locked.

'I'm fine. I just need some water,' she said, her voice muffled slightly.

I sat on the bed and watched the news. After about ten minutes Anna came out quietly coughing and put her head in my lap. Her face disappeared behind hair. I felt her cold lips brush against my hand. Her breathing told me she was drifting off so I watched the headlines roll in and out. I watched graphics of regions without any audio. I tried to relate them to the wider picture in my head. Tried to guess the neighbours, the old empires, the old names for places and that was how I drifted off myself.

2

I ORDERED A WALL map from Amazon for £25.50. It was a physical map with clear variations of shading. These were mainly greens or browns on land showing the contours and terrain of different parts of the world. The mountain ranges were the darkest. The Himalayas and Karakoram mountains loomed like a birth mark over China and India. I also bought a 17th-century map, as a counterpoint, to stick on the adjacent wall. It had come up in recommendations. This map had two circles, one showing Europe, Asia and Africa, the other the Americas. I liked it because the earth had been cracked in two like a nutshell.

If you stood close to the wall looking at them they completely swallowed you up.

Annabel drove us both into work on Monday. She waited for me in the car whilst I carefully rolled up the map and placed it back in its cardboard tubing. I got in and brushed some beer packaging off the front seat. She smirked. The drive was our usual exchange of passive-aggressive comments about the radio. Except for when I put the map, in its tube, on the backseat. She turned the radio down and asked me what it was for. I told her it was a map for my classroom and she stopped short of saying *You're not a geography teacher*. She narrowed her eyes though.

'Why?' she said.

'I want the kids to be able to put things in context. To think about things on a bigger scale than they do,' I said.

'That's sweet,' she said. 'I hope they don't ruin it for you.'

We turned into Eastfield Drive, a genteel cul-de-sac. She pulled into an empty gravel drive and turned the car back around. I leant over to kiss her. She giggled and kissed me back, squeezing the inside of my leg. I undid my seatbelt and looked at the netted windows of the houses around us before opening the car door.

'Don't forget this' she said, pulling the tube from the back.

Her Peugeot drove off and smoothly exited. I reached the roadside on foot just in time to see her pull into the next turn-in, through the school gates. Sometimes if I walked too fast I caught her up in the car park and blew our act. Once I said hello to her, walking past, as she was locking the driver's door. She wasn't impressed. She rolled her eyes when we were undressing that night and said *What's the point, Matt? You might as well shag me on the bonnet.*

Both of us, early on in the relationship, thought we needed to keep it secret. Perhaps I thought I was going to mess her around. I slowed my walking pace, paying attention to the paving stones and the litter fringe to my right. Groups of school kids were starting to appear in sidestreets and at bus stops. When I did eventually come to the school fence I could see clearly across the car park. Annabel was a black and white figure in the distance, going in through the front doors. She worked behind the reception. I was a history teacher.

Mrs Yeoman was the deputy head. That Monday she watched

me staple the top of the map to the classroom's back wall. I was standing on one of my tables. It was a rare period of my weekly timetable when you wouldn't stumble on the stuffy huddle of a sixth-form sociology class. They had my room sometimes and usually pushed my tables together. They appeared to dedicate most of their lessons to micromanaging furniture.

'Have you got a minute, Matt?' Mrs Yeoman said.

I got off the table and put the staple gun down.

'We're in a bit of bother at the moment with Helen off on long-term sick . . .'

She wanted me to reconsider playground duty. To steer the kids away from each other. Adjust their little sails and set them off again in opposite directions. That was not how it would be, so the answer was always, kindly, no. She was a tough nut though. She kept telling me I wasn't the new guy any more.

'You know the routine, the syllabus and a lot of the kids now. I've looked at the rota alongside your timetable. I've earmarked Mondays and Thursdays for lunchtime duties. It shouldn't disrupt any lessons,' she said.

I hesitated. I was running a lunchtime club every Thursday. Those long, sodden winter months wore the kids down and they welcomed the chance to stay inside and sit in front of a television. Some of the other teachers ran clubs at break time but I found twenty minutes wasn't long enough to show them anything of value. I experimented with a few names but settled on the relatively straightforward 'History Club'. Names with Soviet overtones came and went. I thought of taking the crucifix off the classroom wall and fixing a picture of Franz von Papen there, even if it only stayed up for half an hour.

There was no point trying to get the kids to read the textbooks or make period costumes. There was a simple concept to stick to. We met and we watched films. I thought that if I volunteered enough Hollywood films to catch their attention I could sneak in one or two they wouldn't watch otherwise. In truth, for that first month or so, all the historic material we looked at was groomed for the big screen.

I explained the activities I had organised to Mrs Yeoman. She went over to the TV set and brought down the pile of DVDs that were stacked alongside it. I tried to explain the success of History Club whilst she scanned the front of a DVD case.

'They've responded well and six of them came along last week.'

'During the lunch hour?' she interrupted. 'Matt, you haven't cleared this with me. Break times and after-school clubs are OK but legally we can't disrupt the kids' lunch hour. Plus, we are supposed to know, for obvious reasons.'

I told her that I wouldn't be able to get these kids to stay behind after school. Most of them brought their lunch up with them. What was wrong with them sitting in the room and watching the films whilst they ate? As far as censorship was concerned, I thought that it couldn't be any worse than what-ever they saw at home. And if they lacked parental guidance there, in our classroom they could rely on my sarcastic running commentary, one that reminded them of the wisdom of the cutting-room floor.

Just as our discussion began to get heated I turned to see two of the kids standing in the doorway. If they were attentive to the nature of our argument they didn't show it. They stood inexpressively. There was a good chance they heard Mrs Yeoman's first name – Sarah. She hated the kids knowing that. As if to right this wrong she turned sideways on and nodded towards them, clearly flustered.

'I guess this must be another instalment of History Club,' she said.

It was actually detention. They had arrived to help me put up the map. As I countered, Mrs Yeoman decided to take her leave, letting her hand float towards the map and issuing a rebuke to the girls, getting their names wrong then correcting herself. 'Get on with it then, girls. Don't let me see you here again after school.'

One of the girls was vexed at this and started moaning, insisting I'd held her back instead of others. Sometimes, admittedly, I reined her in because I knew I wouldn't have to chase after her friend if I kept both of them back. She suffered for her conscience. In another time she might have thrown herself under a horse.

On Thursday I caught Alex Blake defacing the map. That day the school's headmaster, Wolfencrantz, had asked me personally to cover playground duty. Mrs Yeoman had gone over my head. During my first lesson a group of year 7s had been outside the door passing signals in some strange whispered language, accompanied by gestures, to my pupils through the window. I kept going out there to threaten them. So by the time I caught Alex Blake writing on the map I was at the end of my tether.

His partner in crime, the foil to his wit, was busy distracting me with endless questions. They were questions about a set of questions I had given out. It was a basic summary of a month of work on the Treaty of Versailles. I don't know what Papal infallibility had to do with the post-war conference but he was obsessed with uniting the two issues. Was the Pope at the Palace of Versailles? Why wasn't the Pope at the Palace of Versailles? Had he been invited? Rusty as I was on the Vatican City and the role of the Pope during the wars, I didn't think he warranted a place at the table.

I saw Alex writing on the back wall. He was leant against Egypt whilst trying to craft something onto the map. Even when a general murmur circulated and he knew I was looking, he didn't stop. Instead he muttered *shit* and finished off the contribution. I was so angry I threw a textbook down on my desk and sent papers flying. I immediately gave Alex an hour-long detention and only checked the damage as everyone left.

After scanning the map for a while I realised he had sketched a penis on Israel. When I confronted him later he denied the whole thing at first. In detention he confessed. 'I didn't draw it. I just circumcised it.'

I looked closely at Israel. Its borders with Jordan and Egypt tapered to a point and someone had drawn over these lines to make a penis shape. Then they had gone back and added the balls, which were much less angular. A scissor line of semen flew into the Red Sea. All of these lines were drawn with a black ballpoint pen but the penis head had been drawn over with red pen, showing the coronal ridge. I turned around and Alex was flicking aimlessly through his textbook. I gave him ten minutes of detention then let him out early. I didn't mention the incident again but I wrote a note about it on my class list, next to Alex's name.

~

When I started at St Edwards they gave me a print-out of my classes, a list of the pupils' names with a photo next to each one. I have a terrible memory so it served its purpose. But after a girl was taken by a school janitor and killed, her mom fought for some new laws to reduce risk to kids. Within a few days of the new academic year they came and took my class list off me and gave me one without photos. I found I could remember them by drawing my own impressions of the kids in the gaps between their names, as well as listing certain attributes or features.

I tried to keep this sheet safe. Certainly, I did not want Andre Miller to know that he was 'clubfooted' and, as Leon Monk asserted, 'too quiet to be trusted'. Leon himself 'answered in equivocation' and had a slight 'bung eye'. Still, I don't doubt Leon was as taken aback as me when we learnt that Andre had been found with a knife on him, on the school grounds, during half-term. The caretaker saw him sharpening it on the perimeter fence. He had the other arm through the fence, hanging it there like a pendulum. I asked Leon once, candidly, when I held him back for detention, if he knew whether Andre had it in for one of the teachers, any in particular.

'I don't think so,' Leon said, ruling a margin on a new page. 'He hated all of you.'

I went in to discuss this with the headmaster. Wolfencrantz rapped his fingers on the desk when I told him about Leon's comment. He said, 'The young man could do with going a few rounds every other night – southpaw, I was. Boxing would give him the physique he needs for his self-esteem. He wouldn't have the energy to walk three miles and cross the playing fields during half-term either. He wouldn't want to. Why would a youngster do something like that? It baffles me, Matthew, it really does.'

The police were called and went over to a concrete walkway behind some nearby shops where Andre had last been sighted. Wolfencrantz waited calmly for them to arrive in the school's reception. He shook three officers' hands and told them, 'I used to box.' A circle of deputies gathered around him. He led the police to the meeting room behind the desk. When he tried to open the security door, he forgot to run his staff card across the sensor. He kept yanking the handle regardless. This went on until one of the receptionists craned over their desk, saw the blood rushing to his temples and buzzed him through.

Despite most of Wolfencrantz's colleagues knowing that he had had a penchant for boxing in his twenties, only rumours gave us any context for this. One of my favourites was that he boxed at the Salford Lads' Club, the one made famous by The Smiths, with Morrissey posing in front of the dilapidated building. Wolfencrantz wouldn't have played up this association. We knew he had grown up in a rough area of Britain, but whether it was Salford, Moss Side, Handsworth, Bow or Walthamstow, it really didn't matter. He came from all of them and none of them. He came from a generation that captured self-cultivation. So he bled on the mat and read colonial literature, stuff like *Kings Solomon's Mines*, and his approach was to intimidate people with either of these habits, alongside his slow but sure delivery of English.

His lack of a regional accent was the most cultivated thing

about him. I remember his dismissive laughter when a new teacher asked him where he skied in the holidays.

He was on my interview panel. He offered me a drink. I don't remember anything of the others. I directed my answers to Wolfencrantz because he kept nodding and smiling. The invitation to interview said there would be the Headmaster, the Department Head and some sort of pupil advocate in the room with me. I told my friends it went terribly. Wolfencrantz seemed impressed but I thought he was the advocate.

It turned out that Wolfencrantz was to St Edward's Secondary what Franz von Papen was to the Weimar Republic. In the same way that Papen underestimated Hitler and gave him a foothold in power, Wolfencrantz sacrificed his own influence to a shocking deputy. I was under no illusion – and I don't think he was in the end – that Mrs Yeoman wanted his chair, his office, the respect he had from staff and ultimately his salary and flexible hours. Wolfencrantz was happy to let her run the school to the letter of every guideline sent from Government. She pinballed around, chasing down kids, blowing her top before she understood any given situation, generally shitting herself about everything. And she had it in for me. Not before I had it in for her.

It was Mrs Yeoman who took back my class list with the pictures. She came with a walkie talkie clipped to her belt. She folded the sheet curtly and put it in a file with all the others. It was Mrs Yeoman who pushed for Andre Miller's expulsion before she had even sat down in the case meeting. She seemed to demonise everything he had ever done, which was not much, not much fighting, not a lot of pranks, almost no homework. Andre became a demon for doing nothing at all till he brought that knife out with him at half-term. And god knows, when Social Services went into that house they found a whole lot of nothing there too, no food, no toiletries, no recognisable parenting.

I was telling Annabel all of this whilst she grated carrot into a small bowl. Her flat was warm. She had her back to me. Sweat clung to her shoulders. She was in her vest again. I stood up on my chair and pushed open the window. Then I closed the exercise book in front of me with its tatty handwriting. It went back on my pile. Annabel paced back and forth, looking for things to put in the salad, thinking.

'Who's Franz von . . . *Whatsit?*' she said.

'Papen. He was the guy I told you about. He got off at Nuremberg.'

She shrugged. She pulled the plastic wrapping off a cucumber and sliced it in half.

'She's definitely got a thing for you,' she said, turning and grinning. 'Mrs Yeoman definitely wants some.'

3

IN THE MEADOWHALL Shopping Centre the mannequins had been draped with tinsel. People dipped their heads reverently, as if they were passing an altar. In fact, they were the last shoppers of those late openings, rushing to catch the remaining buses or trams back into town.

Annabel pushed a bag into my hand and looked for her car keys. We were getting some shopping before we made a trip to the coast that weekend. It was three or four days before Christmas. Her family had regularly gone to Scarborough for Christmas breaks as well as during the summer. She asked if we could go again this year. Annabel was in one of her stranger moods the night we set off. She was trying on spontaneity.

'I don't fancy that drive tomorrow morning. You know what, Matt, let's just drop this stuff at my flat and leave tonight. I don't think I'll be able to sleep anyway. Do you care if we can even get a hotel?' she said.

We got back to the flat and picked up some badly packed bags. My toothbrush got tangled in my joggers. A razor clipped a page of a novel Annabel was reading. She threw towels at me, flannels and a squash racket. After this whirlwind of gathering, she disappeared. I found her in the kitchen, standing on a chair in darkness. Her lithe silhouette was leant against the frame of the tiny window. She was looking down onto the street.

'I lied earlier,' she said. 'It's because I like driving at night.'

Her voice cracked a little. I asked her if she was sure she wouldn't be too tired.

'I don't know. I can wake myself up.'

My eyes adjusted to the dark. I could see exactly where the grain of the chair ended and her legs began. I felt my way to the table, pulled myself up and stood on the chair with my arms wrapped around her. She moved forwards a little to accommodate me. Out of the window you could see a snatch of undergrowth by the side of the road. One shadow paced by and ghosted into the bus stop. The lamplight cast a milky film over the night. I was staring at the freckles on her neckline more than anything.

She got dressed quickly and ran both our bags down to the car. Then she rushed back into the room and landed in my lap. I was watching an episode of *Come Dine With Me* that had been filmed in Finsbury Park. A woman was cooking for the other contestants in her basement. As the woman opened a pressure cooker, Annabel began kissing me. Her mouth tasted metallic, her lips cold. When I went down to the car there was a can of Red Bull on the dashboard. I held it for most of the journey, making sure it didn't spill. When she tapped my leg I passed it to her and she took a few swigs.

She told me about the last trip to Scarborough. Her dad's back was getting so bad that it looked like he wasn't going to keep his job. Every time he climbed in the car he let out a pain-filled grunt. He had the seat set vertically, almost tilted forward over the wheel. In the hotel he sat around all day watching

TV. Annabel and her mom went down to the seafront. They offered to stay but he waved them off.

'Just go, I promised I'd bring you. No use coming to the coast just to sit in a hotel room.'

The two of them went out there and practically forgot there was anyone else in their party. Annabel was looking in a rockpool, collecting shells, when she heard her mom scream. She had taken her shoes off and stuffed the socks inside. Out where the waves were just breaking, she was wading and bracing herself for their impact. She had rolled up her leggings. That beach was all pebbles. Annabel slipped over, trying to catch up with her mom. The rocks pressed into her heels. Later, they went for dinner and her mom asked her about the boys in her class. Without her dad around she acted differently.

'Your father wanted a son, you know,' her mom said. 'I'm so glad we had you. I know it's selfish but I wanted a girl so I had someone to talk to.'

Most of the things on the menu were in Italian so her mom told her the dishes to pick. She also ordered large glasses of red and pushed them over to Annabel when the waiters were out of sight. She told Annabel how selfish and unfaithful her grandfather had been. She told her details about her grandad's life that didn't make sense. Her dad was asleep when they got back.

'I learnt most of what I know about my family from that last holiday,' Annabel said. 'I learnt how much they needed to keep secrets.'

Before that night, all their holidays had been a succession of stupid arguments about what time they were going to have dinner. Every year she befriended other kids who were staying in their seafront hotel.

'I told this boy I'd kiss him with tongues if he gave me a pound to play Street Fighter,' Annabel said. 'I played as E Honda and the boy watched me lose four times. He waited there, for the kiss, but I kept asking him if he had any more money.'

Annabel laughed. I shook my head. Her charms might have kept the boy in tow, feeding her his finger-smudged 50p coins, but losing so many fights as E Honda was unthinkable. All she had to do was 'the hundred hand slap'. I explained to her that you got that move by repeatedly pressing punch. I don't know why she hadn't resorted to button-bashing. In the event of doubt and, feeling especially put upon, your only option is to button-bash. Her attention started to drift and she reached for the radio.

'How could you lose with E Honda?' I said and kept shaking my head.

From the seafront, we could see the dark outline of the castle's keep up on the cliff. Then the rest of it formed out of the darkness. We both went quiet and watched the brooding landscape. Instead of finding somewhere to park, Annabel just kept driving around the town. She let the wheel slip back through her palms after every turn, seeming to just enjoy the sensation. An Audi passed us and flashed its lights.

'He's just turned around,' Annabel said.

'Maybe this isn't a good idea.'

'I'm just driving, stop worrying.'

'Oh, well, now he's following us.'

She eyed her wing mirror. 'Let him, he's not going to ram us off the road.'

'And when are we going to sleep? Now we have someone following us.'

'Do you need to sleep? I don't need to sleep. There's plenty we can do.'

The car came to a set of traffic lights. There was a screech of tyres as the Audi pulled out from behind us and into the adjacent lane. The driver turned towards us and lowered his window. He gestured for Annabel to do the same. We could see him more clearly now. He had cheeks raked with acne scars. A hand with a gold ring or two tried to prompt us with little circles in the air. Seeing no reaction, he stopped gesturing but kept his eyes trained on Annabel, his lips on the verge of a smile. There was the sound of a door clicking. Someone got out of the backseat, someone who had been out of view.

'Let's get the fuck out of here.'

'The door's locked!'

The other man was now leant against our car. We could see his white T-shirt underneath a leather jacket. He was pulling the door handle. Then he crouched down and gave the window a wry knock. Annabel gave him two fingers back. She revved the engine as he kicked the side of the car. Before we ran the red light he had another kick, this time at the wing mirror, and managed to take it off. It scuttled underneath us. Annabel was laughing as she sped through the empty streets, whipping past arcades and bus shelters. She looked over at me.

'You were shitting yourself.'

She let the steering wheel straighten out. It slipped through her hands after a sharp right turn. Her finger was still pointing towards me. She brought it down and found my leg, which she patted.

'We almost got carjacked,' I said.

'I know. The door was locked though. Wasn't it exciting?'

'Wasn't it fucking stupid?'

'No . . . of course it wasn't – I knew I had you here to protect me.' When she laughed this time, she patted my cheek. I brushed her arm away.

'You actually wanted to hang out with those guys, didn't you?'

She pulled away. 'What's that supposed to mean?'

'It means that must have felt like a trip down memory lane.'

'Well, fuck you too . . .' she said. After a long pause she added, 'We need to find somewhere to park.'

When we pulled over, I could see the stub of the mirror had two or three wires hanging out of it. She had to look over her shoulder as she reversed into a space along a street just off one of the main roads through town. We were in front of some proud terraced houses. The pavement was lined with grey bins. As she switched the engine off I sat wishing we had some keys to one of those houses. It was about 5am.

'Your mirror is broken.'

'I know.'

She started adjusting the stub. The wire twisted and swung in the darkness. It was like a phantom limb now. There was something pathetic about the slow whirring that started when she turned the switch.

At the age of seventeen Annabel worked Saturday shifts at a newsagents by a traffic island. After work Corinne caught the bus with her and they went back to Annabel's house. They passed her father watching TV. Corinne helped her put on the concealer and mascara. She checked herself out in the mirror and adjusted her white bra. Corinne rushed her out the door. They put their alcohol in plastic Coke bottles. They met up with some local lads. She tagged along for joyrides in their modified cars.

More than once this ended with one, or both, walking home in the cold in a mini-skirt. I don't know whether Annabel got scared about being left on a kerb, watching the car pull away with all the exciting people in it, watching them speed towards a dual carriageway and out of sight. Maybe she did.

A newsagent told us that a severe weather warning had been issued for the north-east. He said this cold front was coming in from Russia. We checked into our bed and breakfast under a steady drizzle. When we walked down to the seafront the rain went crazy. Small huts lined the promenade and ducking into one meant sudden proximity to strangers. We stood, watching the water streaming off the corners of the roof, alternately swelling and thinning again. Then we took our chances and moved on.

I told Annabel that I didn't mind severe weather. I wanted it to snow. I had always wondered what snow would look like over the sea and on the beach. Further across the promenade two homeless-looking men stood at a cockle stand. One made a vain effort to cover his tangled hair with some newspaper. The other might have been bartering but we were too far off to hear anything but raised voices.

We went to a Wetherspoons and waited inside. The staff seemed surprised to have customers. Soon after we sat down they forgot about us. A group of waitresses talked openly near our table. When a thick-set man emerged from a door and put two plates of food on the bar, one of the girls said, 'Who's that for?'

We walked down a street, passing two or three greasy spoon cafes, and stopped in front of an amusement arcade. Beyond the four-seater tables, and past the girl serving, nervously biting her nails by the till, the lighting changed to horizontal bars with an orange glow. These hung over a few sombre slot machines. One old man was slumped into the stool, feeding coins into the machine. He looked up and through us.

Annabel was sure the place we were looking for was on that street but it definitely didn't appear to have been turned into one of the cafes. The wrong shape, the wrong feel, she said. Eventually, whilst we were sheltering outside a novelty shop, pressing ourselves out of the reach of the rain and against the creaking plastic of a rubber dingy suspended from the extended roof, she spotted the relic of an old sweet shop, now a Subway. She recognised the shape of the old building and touched the wall with affection.

'I used to come in here before we'd go to the cinema. I always got those hard-boiled sweets, cola, or rhubarb for my dad.'

I was feeling really hungry by then. The smell drifting out was making me worse. I asked her if she wanted to look inside. She managed to reconstruct the sweet shop whilst we queued. She told me where the floor-to-ceiling fridges had been, where there was a cleaning cupboard and where that had extended straight through into the owner's house. It had surprised her once when he turned around to grab at some dead air on the shelf – a missing tub. Then he lurched out and she saw he had a prosthetic leg. That was why there was always a walking stick propped up behind him and a handrail fixed to one wall. He went back and was gone for five minutes before he found what he was looking for.

She had asked then, in a brash way, what had happened to his leg. Her mom crossed the store and quickly reprimanded her. The guy shrugged and said *It's fine*. But it wasn't fine enough to give her an answer.

We were heading to a cinema by the south beach. Back then, Annabel said, it only had one screen. Somehow it had survived like that. Mr Levermore, in braces and a rippled flannel-shirt, would be leant over the counter slumped into his hand until someone arrived. Then he would give a synopsis of the film they were screening at the time, summarising the action sequences with his own voice-overs. There was rarely anyone stationed at the popcorn stand so Levermore himself got her popcorn. She asked for one tub and he always gave her two, faking some kind of misunderstanding then saying with a shrug, 'Your money is worth twice as much to me.'

When we came to the cinema building Annabel was disappointed to see an amusements sign in red lights. Inside, where the foyer had been, where she could remember Levermore's synopses better than any of the films themselves, a wall had been knocked through. Machines were lined up from corner to dark corner. We split up and realised that there were many, many more people in there than the coast had so far revealed to us. A woman in thick make-up with permed hair glided past me and called out to the staff. I could smell her strong and cheap perfume. She got the worker's attention by going up on her tiptoes and wrapping her fur scarf around the back of his neck. I carried on and walked down the aisles of slot machines.

The men playing, old before their time, were alternately lit up and then plunged into a bleaker darkness. Their eyes broke from communion with the machine to watch me stroll past and I seemed to bring too much of the outside with me. They returned to the lurid colours and lights, coughing or grunting with reticence. The machines made constant noises themselves. There were spurts of phaser fire and recorded sounds of falling money. I was struck by the fact that one large cinema screen had once held everyone's attention. Now attention was divided up between each machine, along each row. All the light was galvanising to the senses but debilitating to the body.

I saw Annabel talking to a worker at the payout desk. I walked over and heard her asking questions. She wanted to know if they had any information about where Mr Levermore was now. The worker listened to her enquiry and said he needed to talk to the manager. I saw a tense conversation between him and another man with long black hair. That man came out next and asked if he could help her.

'I'm looking for a Mr Levermore – do you know how I might be able to track him down,' Annabel said.

'I don't know anyone by that name.'

'Did you buy this place off him? If you don't mind me asking.'

'I don't know anyone by that name but I do mind you asking.'

A woman overheard Annabel's story and walked over to explain the owner's paranoia. She said he was expecting bailiffs from all over the country to find him there eventually. Added to that, there were problems with the tenancy. Don't take it personally, she said. She asked who it was we were trying to get hold of. She didn't recognise the name herself but when Annabel mentioned he had owned the cinema the woman said, as if it were a revelation, 'This used to be a cinema!'

A payout rang through the next aisle. Annabel sat down and watched a punter stumble off with his winnings. Her blonde hair was shady and then orange in the bubblegum glow of the machines. What I didn't realise was that all this renovation was having more than a superficial effect on her. If I had, I might have been more careful with what I said that afternoon.

'What are we doing here?' she said.

'I don't know', I said. 'We're not collecting any winnings, I know that.' I stared over at the machines.

'You mean I'm not. Do you pity me?' she asked.

I didn't understand the question. I left her long enough to pick up her own thread.

'You pity the way I think. Sometimes it's like you're putting up with me, like you think I'm simple. I don't mean dumb-simple, just like . . . I'm kind of basic. Simple way of thinking. That's what *this* is like.'

She had gestured towards the shifting lights of the room.

'You mean hanging around in a casino that's about to be repossessed. I sort of enjoy it,' I said.

'Yeah, I guess you do. Because this is what you want to do anyway, but doing it with someone like me, that makes it OK for you.'

I told her it had been her idea to drive out to the coast.

'It doesn't matter, let's forget it,' she said.

~

I was still waiting on that snow, blown in from Russia. On our way back to the hotel we realised even the rain had stopped. There was the heavy damp along the beach walls that would turn into frost overnight. In our room, Annabel paced around twisting the heater dials over and over, impatient for them to come on. I left her wrapped in a blanket and bought a bottle of bourbon from the bar. Whilst we sipped from plastic cups she played songs from her phone and looked down at the carpet.

'Imagine if you were pulling my clothes off and you saw a tattoo.'

'A tattoo of what?'

'I don't know. A tattoo of anything.' She suddenly went wide-eyed. 'A dragonfly running down my back. How would you feel about that?'

Whilst she left this question hanging in the air, she kept her body entirely out of sight, motionless under the mound of blanket.

'If I hadn't told you, how would you feel?' she said.

'Have you got a tattoo?' I asked.

'No – you saw me naked earlier, or were you thinking of someone else?'

She sipped some of her drink. I laughed.

'I wasn't. I don't do that.'

'Don't you?' She raised an eyebrow and bit into the lip of her cup. 'My point is it's my body and I can change it.'

'So you're thinking of having plastic surgery?'

'No. I don't think so.'

'Are you telling me you're getting a tattoo?'

'I don't know.'

'Because I don't mind dragonflies.'

'That's not the point. You're missing the point.'

She got up then, holding the blanket around her and dropping her empty cup onto the floor. I wanted to look out the window but it was impossible to see anything in the darkness behind the nets. She tucked the woollen blanket into the towel rack with minimal effort. It dropped to the floor. She was nonplussed at this and pulled down her jogging bottoms. She half-turned and tucked her thumb under the hem of her underwear.

When she had stripped completely she sat down on the toilet and looked up at me as the sound of piss hitting the bowl rang out. I could have reached out to her then, across that tiled floor between us. Maybe I should have told her that simplicity, and the basics, were important, that I wasn't scared of that. Instead, I squeezed my plastic cup, watching the level of the bourbon rise as she reached forward and found the door handle. She pushed the door towards me and the pissing sound changed pitch.

About a month or so after Christmas, Corinne gave birth to a boy. She had sent pictures of the scans in silver envelopes. They were addressed to both of us and Annabel kept them on the windowsill or pinned up on the fridge. I didn't really look inside. I looked at the embossed lettering on the cards and wondered who the father was. The news of the birth came on the phone but, of course, Corinne sent a picture of mother and bouncing baby boy not long afterwards, in another silver envelope. I looked at that one. I half expected Seb to be in those pictures, leant against the rails of the hospital bed and smiling proudly, but he wasn't. When I asked Annabel how Seb was doing she seemed distracted.

'He's fine. Fit and healthy. Breastfeeding. 8lb 6oz.'

4

I BEGAN GETTING UP at 5am. I made myself toast and a fruit salad. For about an hour I would prepare to leave the flat. I spent that hour lying on the sofa and listening to the growing sounds of traffic. Franz von Papen's memoirs lay in my lap. Sometimes I read them. Sometimes I just left them there. After a five-minute nap I would claw at my briefcase, sit up and straighten my tie. Then I descended the airy staircase through two floors and crossed the road.

It was a five-minute walk into the city centre and I shortened it to three. I headed for the tram stop. All around me were university buildings with their panelled decor. The library was opposite the station. It was more stately, standing about as tall as a medium-rise, with long glass windows on every other floor. They reflected cloud and showed little of the interior. At that time in the day there were no students around. It was just suits like me.

On the tram I occasionally got a four-seater to myself. That's when I'd spread myself out and pull the battered red hardback out of my briefcase. The memoirs still had a county library sticker on the inside cover. I had already read them but I used to flip to my favourite passages. A few years before the First World War, when he was a military attaché on a trip to Mexico, Papen went to the Northern Provinces, to where the revolutionary bands were really troubling the Mexican government. That particular intrigue ended in Papen being chased and shot at by a soldier in a local citadel. He had only just finished a friendly conversation with the young man and had turned his back to walk away. Franz had no business being there though. I looked up from the yellowed pages and the city centre was gliding by. More people were moving about but all the shops still had their shutters down.

After twenty minutes of travel through the tightly packed streets, the buildings gave way and revealed a more sombre Sheffield. It seemed caught in the valley rising either side. When the tram had cleared the first overpass I put my book away and disembarked by the cramped newsagents with papers on display. The shopkeeper's greeting got warmer every day. I bought a paper, exchanged some pleasantries with him and went to wait at a bus stop. It was twenty minutes on the tram and then another half-hour on the bus.

I thought of Annabel whenever I waited at that bus stop. Looking up at the hills dotted with council flats I thought of the warmth in the passenger seat of her Peugeot. I tried to imagine that seat remaining empty. I couldn't be sure it was. She had told me were on a break. It was worse in the mornings, thinking about that.

Soon enough the bus would arrive and I let anyone else waiting get on first. In the windows wild young faces would emerge out of shadow, with three-year-olds standing on seats, bouncing up and down. At the back schoolkids in blazers were throwing Coke cans at each other. Some of them knew my name. When we got stuck in traffic, the rate of their blows only increased.

And sure enough, once they had got bored of saying my name and giggling every morning, small objects started to hit me on the back of the head. It might have been a single crisp packet or a piece of balled-up notepaper at first but it became pretty regular. They all seemed to hold their breath after the impact. Papen didn't run from that citadel in Mexico because he was a meek soldier frightened by the sound of gunfire. He ran because he had no jurisdiction in the provinces of Mexico. He also, probably, didn't have a firearm.

I remember one day of torrential rain. Everyone rushed onto the bus and sat panting, relieved to be crammed into the lower deck, dripping from their anoraks and umbrellas onto the floor. A tall guy got on and didn't pay. He brazenly stood at the bottom of the stairs when the driver called him back. The driver switched the engine off and said he wasn't going anywhere.

The guy, in his early twenties, wearing a vest, spat onto the floor, mixing phlegm and muddy rainwater with his foot. He explained clearly that he had already shown his daysaver and offered to speak to the driver outside of his cabin. We all sat watching, occasionally looking at the time. When a chorus of boos sprang up from the impatient school kids at the back the tall guy stormed off into the rain, bracing his shoulders against it.

The bus pulled away and we all heard a loud clunk. The guy had kicked the bus, around where the engine was. The kids all jumped up and got excited. It was as if some of them had taken the force of the kick themselves. They didn't shut up about it for the rest of the journey. Amongst the other entertainments were a family made up of about thirteen children and one mother. I never saw them all getting off the bus but I'm sure she lost one or two a day in the process. She could replace them quickly enough. There was of course an almighty, always sweating, fat man. He had a bag full of cassette tapes that I gazed into whenever I had to sit next to him. I think they were motivational tapes.

I went into St Edwards through the main entrance. As I passed the front desk I waved to the receptionist. Mandy was a widow with a flat top of tightly curled black hair. She had lived in Sheffield all of her life and had excellent elocution. Sometimes I glimpsed Annabel moving between offices in the background. Everyday Mandy said hello back to me and told me if I had any post. Annabel opened a filing cabinet and asked Mandy where she could put the paperwork. She looked at me and always gave a half-smile. We were on an indefinite break.

The map loomed over me between lessons. From my desk I could see Eastfield Drive over a row of oak trees. It was a quiet cul-de-sac with identical, sand-coloured houses curving around an island of poorly laid tarmac. There were still one or two cars parked in the drive in the daytime. People in oversized T-shirts would come out and move the cars out of the drive or into the drive. I didn't know why. My gaze often settled over there, out of that window in the corner of the room. It was half covered by a blind descending from the ceiling that rattled whenever a door slammed in the next room. Because some of my worst kids would gravitate to that window-seat during lessons, they thought I was giving them the evils. I was just staring though.

After 3pm, when St Edward's exhaled all of its pupils,

every corridor of the school seemed to relax. That was when I sat down to my class lists. I would spread them out in front of me, shuffling the pages backwards and forwards to try and remember events of the passing weeks. Shaun Rafter, one Thursday morning, had landed a punch on his classmate's arm and tried to kick him out of his chair. The fight didn't get very far and had arisen out of some perceived slight that had been written on Shaun's notepaper. When I tried to get to the bottom of it I found the offending page had been ripped out and cast into the ether, probably out of the corner window. I looked down onto the portakabin roof below and saw numerous things: pens, condom wrappers and lots of balled-up notepaper. When I spoke to Shaun alone I advised him to learn to control his aggression. He sighed, got out his mobile phone and started for the door. He told me he was ringing his mother.

I wrote *Will grow up to kick buses* by Shaun's name on the class list. Then I crossed out 'buses' and put 'automobiles/anything'. Shaun would kick any machine. I daresay he would kick a pram or a wheelchair if it got a rise out of him. There are people who feel their anger like that. Anything that has direction and momentum, anything going somewhere they are not, is worthy of a few blows.

As for Jodie Tatham it took me a little while longer to nail it. My entry for her was the result of general perception rather than an actual event. For instance, whenever I told her to stop turning around she'd go bright red and pull the neck of her jumper partly over her face. She was a little paranoid that people were talking about her all the time and it got her into a muddle. She had also wrinkled her nose a few times when I was talking about the Middle East. I recalled her dad was once a football coach at St Edwards. There was general consensus that with his constant masquerading in a St George's shirt, his aversion to ethnic players and his emphasis on long-ball football, Jodie's father was a BNP-sympathiser. For Jodie I had to capture this pride. I put *The inevitable product of an overachieving island nation.*

Charlotte Baines was *antsier than James Watt. Smart, but probably incapable of contributing to any revolution, industrial or otherwise.*

For Charlotte's sister Kelly I could not bring myself to state the truth, at least not in words. Instead I drew a single pram spilling over with babies. I drew a pile of trainers behind. I added to that pile whenever I was stuck for something else to write.

An hour later and the cars had come back to fill up Eastfield Drive. They covered most of the tarmac. I leant against that corner window, opening and closing the blinds that hung further up. Before leaving I'd scan the map from corner to corner. The southern hemisphere was in a dire state. Graffiti covered a little bit of every continent and scrawled figures were bunching up in the sea. I smudged some of the markings with my thumb. There was a blue smear across my hand and I held it up into the light. Before the caretaker could arrive at the top of the stairs I collected up my class lists and packed them into my desk drawer. After I locked it I pulled at the handle, just to be sure.

Alex Blake and his scrawling on the world map came back to me months after the incident. One day in March I sent two year 7s with a message for Mr Lancet, a teacher who used my room on Fridays. When they didn't come back I left my class to look for them myself. They weren't in the playground or the sports hall. I mounted the staffroom stairs to see if anyone had noticed them wandering around, doe-eyed and suggestible. By the staffroom there was a noticeboard which was usually empty. That day a page of scuffed notebook paper pinned there caught my eye. I recognised the terrible handwriting. A set of squashed numbers ran down the side and people's names were written alongside these.

Shaun Rafter.

Mrs Yeoman.

Pythagoras.

Some of the names were incomprehensible but most of them were teachers. A few numbers had no name assigned to them as if those places were still under deliberation. I pulled the note off and went into the kitchenette, where Greg Cope, a Maths teacher, nodded at me and put a sandwich on the side. I asked him why the paper was up there.

'This is the much fabled *Hit List*. Apparently it got pulled off a year 10 in Angela's class.'

'Year 9,' I said. 'It's Alex Blake's.' I knew this because I could recognise the kid's handwriting anywhere. It was so distinctly looping and messy I couldn't see his test papers being accepted by the exam board next year. That was unless we could get permission for him to type them. I tapped the paper and looked up at Greg. 'What is it meant to be a list of? What is it for?'

'You know, who he's going to kill first, with a machete or a Beretta.' Greg briefly simulated a Valentine's Day massacre shootout and sprayed bullets against the far wall then stopped abruptly. 'God knows.'

I pointed to number 2 which was Mrs Yeoman's position. 'This is brilliant.'

'Yeah, it also might be police evidence soon, so you'd better leave it on the board. Sarah is taking it seriously in light of . . .'

In light of Andre Miller. The boy had disappeared in a veil of social services and police intervention. All that might be left of him was a 'fuck you' which had ripped through part of Antarctica on my classroom wall. Greg saw the enjoyment I was getting out of Mrs Yeoman's unpopularity and hastened to point out my name was also on the list. I was annoyed, surprised, to see it there, albeit in the lower regions at number 19. I laughed to make a point of not feeling threatened. Then I tucked the list into my shirt pocket. Greg took an eager bite and shook his head. He waved the sandwich at me.

'Matt, I wouldn't mess with her on this one.'

'Why?' I held the list up. 'You've got to agree going to the police is ridiculous.'

He shrugged and began laughing. This was probably for my benefit. I knew if anyone was looking for the note he wouldn't hesitate to point them in my direction.

I was planning to put the Hit List back once common sense had prevailed at the school. At that moment I put it in the back pocket of my trousers and buttoned it. I was marking coursework at my flat when I remembered it again. I had decided to put a wash on and threw my trousers in as an afterthought. In the time it took me to load the washing machine from a cracked basket, roll a cigarette on the sideboard, make a cup of coffee and traipse across the wooden flooring to sit under the halo of my desk lamp, I remembered the Hit List.

I was picking through an overwritten paragraph about the Black Panthers and the infamous Olympic salute when it came to me, as if it was scrunched in the black-gloved hand of the athlete. In fact the list was still folded and inside the machine. The 45-degree water was soaking through the cotton and obliterating the paper faster than the ink could run. When I pulled it out desperately, a few minutes into the spin cycle, the paper was ripped. After it had dried on the radiator the writing looked inhuman, like blobs of oil residue.

I sat down on a chair that was propping the door open. My washing machine was crammed into a little utility room at the back of the flat. I pulled up my satchel and found my notebook and a pen. I tried to fake the list on the notepaper but I couldn't remember all the rankings. I also couldn't get my handwriting that bad. It seemed too obviously me. I was fucked unless I could get Alex to write it out again.

I abandoned my form and tried to find him in the IT suite the next morning. I ran in on the wrong class and as I backed out, barely explaining myself, I walked into a printer. The teacher paused and narrowed her eyes at me. A row of children turned away from her and watched my frantic button pressing. The printer was wheezing out blank sheets of paper, and giggles spread through the class. In that sea of faces there was no Alex Blake.

I tried to compose myself on the edge of another room full of sixth formers until eventually I was drawn to the windows and the grey playground below. Amongst the milieu of painted lines, a spread of intersections crossed by groups of kids, there was a large and dangerous-looking figure. So much action flowed towards him, lines of kids chasing, and then, as the figure came to a standstill, rippling away like they felt the force of a great stone dropped amongst them.

In a long suede coat that whipped up their exuberance, Wolfencrantz was supervising the playground football. It was hard to tell when he had the ball as his form eclipsed it. He seemed to make it invisible at his feet and would show it in flashes now and then to maintain their commitment to the game. For a while I watched him meander around the playground and I suspected he hadn't even nominated an end that he was shooting towards. He took one look up and produced a rugged chip, all he could do with the weathered, deflated ball they played with, to the set of goals he had just been turned away from.

The pass bounced amongst a few kids scattered towards the backpost. It looked inventive but pointless. Either no one had read it or no one accepted him as a viable inclusion to the game. Then a boy peeled out of the shadow of a beanpole sixth former who was idly watching. The neck of this boy's jumper was wrenched back on one side by the strap of a satchel. He quickly ducked under the strap and threw the bag to the ground. As he stepped sideways he took the ball on his chest, leant backwards and it sat up perfectly for him to hit in the air.

Wolfencrantz's presence again quickly asserted itself on the playground. He unloaded a barrage of firm handclaps to the goalkeeper who had pulled off an unlikely save. This was whilst Wolfencrantz still took kicks on each ankle. The kids either thought the ball was still there or wanted to take advantage of a rare chance to kick an adult. When the keeper punted the ball high a few minutes later Wolfencrantz called the boy who had hit the sweet volley to the fringes of the game. He put his ancient hand on the boy's shoulder and gave him a few words.

I did not find Alex and later Mrs Yeoman did not believe I had done anything but intentionally destroy the Hit List. Her face was flooded with indignation when she heard I'd taken and lost it. She asked me for the keys to my desk. After I declined several times, she swore and I closed the door of my classroom, telling the waiting pupils to return to the foot of the stairs.

I watched her hand shake as she tried to get the key in the desk's lock. Eventually I took over, unlocked it myself and we stared down into the open draw. There was a picture of Franz von Papen on top of my papers. It was taken when he served as the German Ambassador to Turkey. He was wearing a garish combination – a black striped bow tie with a pinstripe jacket. He looked like an old Hammer Horror actor from the fifties, a bit Vincent Price, with a barely noticeable moustache. The hairs were white at the ends like a fir branch under snow. It would be impossible for Mrs Yeoman to know the significance of that glossy picture. I tried to second guess her thinking and settled on the idea she thought we were looking at a picture of my grandfather.

'Is that Vincent Price?' she asked.

'Yes.' I hesitated. 'I found it when I moved my stuff in.'

She started going through the papers. I helped by gathering bundles and placing them on the desk. At the bottom of the draw there was nothing but Tesco receipts and a few shirt buttons. As she leafed through the papers, I restated my innocence. Soon after, she pulled out my own class list. She mouthed a name and comment with barely a whisper of sound.

'Jodie Tatham – *the inevitable product of an overachieving island nation . . .* what is this?'

I think, rightly, that in all her imperiousness over the school, Mrs Yeoman was quite a vulnerable soul. She had not pursued the list with Alex's guilt in mind, but with mine. As it happened two lists had been compiled. Alex was not alone in making wild projections of thought and feeling. Mrs Yeoman was too embarrassed to look at my class list for any notable length of time and folded it in half, as she had folded the first.

When she next spoke it was clear she had little to say.

'Matthew, I've been thinking about the map.' She stood looking at the wall, not aghast, but contemplating the map in a way I had wanted the kids to. Her mouth shrank to the size of a small coin. 'It looks tatty and there are some lewd things drawn here.' Then she moved closer to the Middle East. Her faint shadow began to climb the wall. 'Matt, some of the things on this map are quite racist.'

During the Easter holiday I went into school and took the map down. With the commotion I had made over putting it up, I didn't want the pupils to see it taken away from them.

I had to call the caretaker to get him to open my room. He got to the top of the stairs and made a *hmph* sound when he saw the door.

'You're up in the satellite room, eh?'

That is what he had christened this energy-saving construction. He put the large set of keys, brimming like a jailor's, back in the pocket of his overalls.

'You know this room is energy-saving?' I said.

He passed me a newer key, with a grey plastic handle – it looked like the key for a shed. Then he said. 'You mean it's cheaper to heat.'

Before he left he mentioned that it was the second time he had opened up during the holiday.

'This room?' I asked.

Apparently the sociologists had been in there again. A sixth former had left her textbook behind. I walked over to my desk and checked the drawer was still locked. The sovereignty of my desk had already been violated by Mrs Yeoman. The lists were gone but I didn't want anyone else rooting around, looking at that picture of Papen. Nothing had been moved or changed. The desks were laid out in their neat rows. The chairs were tucked in behind them. It was left for me to make the changes.

First I set myself up on a chair so I could reach the top of the map. I had a blunt knife that I'd brought from my flat. Starting on the eastern side and working westwards, I began plucking the staples from each side, wrenching some of the trickier ones out with the knife. Eventually the map began to fold over and collapse under its own weight. When I came face to face with Andre Miller's 'fuck you' over the sea-fringed white of Antarctica, I tried not to take it personally.

At some point I realised I was not alone. I heard gentle echoes on the stairs. I thought the caretaker might have decided to lock up early. Stepping down from the chair I turned to see Annabel, in full office attire, enter and pause nervously.

'Mandy saw you come in,' she said. 'There are some things I wanted to tell you.'

Annabel was moving to London. It was something she had been thinking about for a good few months. And along with her newfound need for independence, which she had felt so keenly at Christmas, she felt a need to open up new frontiers. I said that it was understandable. I picked the staples up off the floor whilst she spoke. My room had been so clean it felt bad to just leave them there. She asked whether I had been making it into work OK.

'Yeah, fine, I've started getting the tram,' I said.

'All the way?' she asked.

'Well, no, I catch the bus, sometimes.' I threw the staples into the bin. 'But it's nice to be able to catch up on some reading.'

She sat down on top of one of the desks. I moved the chair to the centre of the map. Then I got back up on it, folding parts of the map back so it didn't billow out and wrap around me. She sat there for a few minutes on the other side of the room.

'This probably isn't great timing, Matt,' she said, her voice seeming to get louder as she spoke. 'But, I'm really sorry. It's over.'

5

Two motorbikes pulled into the car park and dragged
fumes in with them. Sunshine poured down on the cars and
families. As I passed between groups, the bike engines died
down. Three or four of my year 11s were pulling back the flaps
of envelopes. There was glad-handing. Mandy called after me
as I passed through the doors. She pressed a note to the reception glass. It was 11am, results were in and I was running late.
The note said that Wolfencrantz wanted to see me after I had
talked to some of the parents.

I walked back out into the car park. There we were, all
together, finally, with nothing to lose. I tried to relax my guard
but I felt like a lot more needed to be said. I found it around
the back of the workshops, on the far side of the building,
where a group of young men were having their last illicit cigarettes. A few of them tried to hide the fag-ends in a cursory
gesture – one put a Marlboro out on the redbrick so I set them
at ease. It was summer after all and they weren't coming back.
In fact, neither was I.

'What, sir?' one asked.

'Yeah, I'm leaving too. I wanted to wish you guys luck,' I
said.

'Wish me luck, sir? You should have given me a C. You can
keep your luck.'

A debate opened up about the merits of my classes. A few voices rose up in my defence.

'Forget him, sir. He is just having a fit because he didn't revise and he told his dad he was gonna go to College. *Hehe-hehe.*'

They then told me how this pupil had devised a decent system of adapting the school reports, firstly by scratching out different parts of the grades with a scalpel he'd taken from a stockroom, then by excruciatingly matching up the right colours of ink, the right thickness of the nib, and shifting lines around or adding them on. If his dad bothered to read the criticisms of the text rather than the grades, if either of his parents penetrated the troubled handwriting, the boy just explained that the teachers were hard on him because they wanted to push him to fulfil his amazing potential.

It was quite funny – knowing that his father was going to take a hand to him for maintaining a consistent and high level of bullshit throughout the year. They told me how at home he was the captain and joint top scorer for the basketball and football teams respectively. Apparently I had told him he should look forward to getting a scholarship after college. Even Wolfencrantz had considered adapting his schedule to give him the private maths lessons that would bring his arithmetic up to scratch with the other subjects. The lies appeared to have mounted up.

I remembered the note Mandy had showed me and excused myself from the smokers.

The car park and playground were draining clean as I went back into the school. I admired the solemn passage of steel columns in the main corridor. I went right through the school to the very back where a staircase looked out, through perspex smudged with dust and fingerprints, onto a range of fauna that ran around the back of the buildings and sectioned it off from the surrounding housing.

This was where the old hub of the school had been run from. They moved most of the offices because it wasn't cost effective to be installing broadband wires and knocking through walls in an old redbrick building. Whilst most of the former offices were filled with stuff no-one had the authority to throw away – I passed an open door with a chipped white exercise bike poking out – the old Head's office had been declared a no-go area. Thus it preserved a thick oak desk towards the tall windows at the back of the room and also a chalkboard mounted on the left-hand wall. That would have been where the smoking boy had his imaginary arithmetic lessons.

This was Wolfencrantz's office. I approached the door on the third floor and gave it a gentle knock. The greeting was immediate, as always, and allayed my fears of a volatile opening. As I pushed the door, I first saw planet earth. It was the centre of a small orrery that rose to waist height. Wolfencrantz was sat behind his desk at the far end. At first I thought he was standing over it. In fact he sat there, with a black pen. He looked about to write something and hesitated.

'Hello, Matthew.' He glanced at his watch. 'Is that the time? The afternoon has disappeared. I'll just finish up. Are you OK to sit down?'

He pointed the pen to the chair. I sat down with my hands quite still and breathed out. Wolfencrantz had done well to maintain the spaciousness of this old haven. I found myself staring sideways at the orrery with my hands between my legs.

With its little golden renderings of the planets, it was both a magnificent and understated thing. Each planet reflected the dull colours of oak as well as the giant frames of his bookshelves. He saw that I was taken with it.

'That was a present from my uncle,' he said. 'I think he was horse trading for a more sizeable one with a friend of his in London when he spotted that on a market stall in Marrakech.'

I told him I had only seen one up close once before. They kept it in the science museum back home. Whilst it was much bigger it didn't seem half as impressive as the one Wolfencrantz had acquired from his uncle. Maybe some of his family were pretty flush after all. I told him I really liked it anyway, and that I'd get one, if I could afford it.

'Well, you can't beat the real thing, can you?' He stamped the floor here, twice and firmly, beneath the table. 'Still,' he said, 'why not embellish it, put it in gold and keep it polished?' Then, as if remembering that I had spoken, too, he placed the pen down on his wad of paper and said the word *home*. 'When was the last time you went back to Birmingham, Matthew?'

'It surprises me that you haven't achieved everything you wanted to. The things we envisaged when you started. Looking at how everything has panned out for the year, it seems you've struggled to settle in. You haven't really asserted yourself in the classroom as we thought you might. Has this been the right post for you? I know you're as disappointed as we all are with the results today. Sometimes you're dealt a bad year but you can't let that impact on you as a teacher.'

His assessment didn't seem fair. For one, my year 7s and 8s were doing quite well. No-one was worried about their performance. Secondly, I felt my relationship with the students was for the most part good, give or take a few disciplinary issues. I told Wolfencrantz I had no problem with the syllabus, even if it was dry at times. I explained that it was the stuff *around* teaching that was bothering me. When it came to the material and the kids I was fine. The exam results had not been great but I was still finding my feet. He didn't seem to listen.

'I know you and Mrs Yeoman have had some working issues this year. It's a problem for all of us if you subvert the chain of command. I think you can acknowledge that.' He drew breath. 'She has her own methods for running the school, but she is under a lot of pressure to perform – we all are.' He sat up a little. 'You say your relationship with the pupils has been healthy?'

I nodded. He bent down and opened a drawer. He pulled out a few sheets and placed them at the edge of the desk so I could read them. He pointed to my handwriting, scrawled around the lists of my classes.

'This does not demonstrate a rapport,' he said. 'There is something I am inherently worried about here.'

He pointed to different comments. Some sentences ran into crammed paragraphs on individual students. Wolfencrantz or Mrs Yeoman had circled the comments they found to be most offensive.

I had stepped into that office ready to accept a parting of ways. The least I wanted was to part with Wolfencrantz on good terms. He had always said things which suggested he saw something in me. Now he made it clear we were beyond the stage of nurturing potential. And he wasn't talking about the kids, he was talking about me. He relayed the stories of the lists but somehow the two had been confused. He believed I was not only responsible for the comments of my class list, but also for the defamation and underlying threat of Alex Blake's Hit List. I tried to straighten this out.

'I was on Alex's list! I was number 19!'

'Well,' he said. 'Regardless of authorship, you destroyed potential evidence.'

Things did not look good at this point. The more I spoke the more I seemed to incriminate myself to Wolfencrantz. Eventually he brought the conversation around to the content which he had found offensive. He wanted to confront statements I had made about individual children. There was a strong argument that those thoughts had compromised my ability to teach the students. He could brush aside the caricatures I had made. Those were the observations about their looks or behaviour which told them apart at the beginning of the year. Superficial judgements were partly natural.

Beyond this there was an abuse of position. He argued that I had segregated them. My judgement had been fundamentally impaired. He asked me to say something in my defence. He asked if there was anything going on in my personal life.

There was a newspaper article I'd read as a teenager that I've never forgotten. Chris Tarrant, in his days as an undergraduate at Birmingham University, had caught a Brent goose and tied its wings together. The details were lost on me. How he'd caught the damn thing. What he used to bind the wings. How he smuggled it through the campus to his halls of residence and then got it up the flights of stairs to an open window. There was no mention either of the outcome – though that was in no doubt. I do remember that he 'threw' the goose from the top floor, still bound.

The more I grew up and saw these kids coming through behind me, the more I thought of him tying those wings together. There are a lot of trouble makers, but there are also a lot of people who we shouldn't be pushing for good grades, exam results, for colleges or university. There are only so many things you can give a kid like that to fail at, till they decide that they don't care either way. I didn't want to detract from Wolfencrantz's personal beliefs in the individual but we were losing more every year. And that's where he cut me off and drew the conversation to a close.

'You,' he said.

I paused and he stared through me for a second whilst he straightened one of his lapels.

'You said "We are losing more every year". I'm correcting you, Matthew. You are losing more every year, or so I would expect if you were able to continue teaching here.'

Annabel was waiting outside the entrance to my flat when I got back. She had lots of make-up on, a new haircut, and she was holding a neatly packed cardboard box of my things. She said she had tried phoning me. About six times over the past two hours. She had left three voicemails. She was moving out of her flat. If she hadn't found me then she would have taken my books and clothes to the Salvation Army. I took the box, went inside and put it under the stairs, hoping none of my neighbours would spot it. Then I walked back out to see if Annabel was still in the car park.

She wasn't.

I went for a walk. I waited by the train station. I circled through the abandoned steel workshops and factories. Posters for discount clubnights were plastered over the brickwork and doors. I caught the tram from the station on my way back through town to the flat. On the same line, in the opposite direction, trams run towards the Meadowhall Shopping Centre. It's a ten- or fifteen-minute ride out of the city centre. I could see the youngsters crowding onto each tram heading that way. They dressed up just to go to Meadowhall in the summer holidays. There are ski-slopes somewhere out that way as well.

BOMB ASSEMBLY

I

It struck me that to stay in Sheffield would be a mistake. I had to let go of the place. A phone call to a friend threw up some names and opportunities; I went with one of them and had a favourable email from the head of a city college in Birmingham. She offered to meet with me and discuss a role that had arisen to teach history to the college students. I took what I could from my years in Sheffield and packed to go back home.

I came into New Street one Friday at around 7.30 in the morning. I had got a call about an interview a few days before. It felt like I'd crossed the Iron Curtain; the platforms have that drab, apologetic concrete that's best consigned to the 1980s. As I moved up the escalator I watched the attendants clearing railings that blocked off certain parts of the adjoining shopping centre at night. They were folded up and wheeled away. I walked through to the far side of the building. I looked through the security doors as the attendants opened them. There were brick walls running into darkness.

I went for a cigarette. I was standing on a small, raised island of concrete at the taxi rank.

No cars were present at the junction, the lights changed without them. I got in a waiting taxi and asked about the fare. The driver could barely hear me but acquiesced with a shrug.

We rolled past familiar buildings. I saw a concrete office block that was being demolished as we ducked into the Queensway. There was only a little traffic and I tipped the driver with the change I had from the station's newsagents. The head did not tell me how many they were interviewing. There was no-one else in the waiting room. They brought me straight through, even though I was early. I'm not sure I was particularly with it but I got a call two days later saying they had the funding to take me on a rolling contract.

The blinds were reeled back in the canteen. The breeze wafted the smell of salted chips through the hallways. Leafy branches flapped in the open windows. The Goths sat around and spoke in broken silences. A pretty girl had settled at the table but she had a bullring piercing in her nose to reassure the others she wouldn't turn socially kosher. The big move was not far off now. I got lunch from the canteen some days and as I queued I took the time to look around the room at everyone.

In a year or two most of the faces would change completely. The college would be seven miles further up the Bristol Road. Campus would move and implications were furthered every week in board meetings. The head esteemed me enough to give me an invitation to one or two. At the second time of asking I actually showed up, coffee in hand. It was a Friday morning and I had a class that afternoon with some A2 students. We were dedicating most of our time in class to running through the previous year's Vietnam papers.

The board meeting took place in the conference room at the back of the college. It looked over some impressive playing fields and an old sign planted in the corner of a pitch which read 'Bomb Assembly Point'. The sign was a bit of an over-sight. I tried to bring it up with Munroe but she was often too busy. I imagined students on their knees, wiring bombs on the windy sports field. I walked back away from the window and tried to dismiss it.

There were about ten or twelve chairs in the meeting room. A screen was unravelled from the ceiling and the cord dangled beneath it. The projector was on and there was a picture of some mountains on the screen. I sat down as four or five colleagues were already in discussion. People were already trying to make their claims to a share of the funding.

Munroe, the college head, greeted me enthusiastically. She came around to my side of the table and put a Dove-creamed hand on my shoulder. She asked about some of the students. A man sitting across from me pushed his glasses up into his face. He got the attention of a fat man next to him and mut-tered something. I assumed we were in the presence of some of the college's governors. Whilst we were talking, one of them produced a magazine from a bag beneath the table and started handing it around.

'Have you seen the *Future Ed* cover this quarter? Guess who is the star attraction.'

'We'll be making it into the *Times Education Supplement* in a week or two.'

'Has anyone spoke to the builders?'

'Any movement on the dates?'

More people filtered into the room and took up the re-maining chairs. The magazine that had everyone smiling was the *Future Education* quarterly. On the front was the headline 'The Brave New Future of College Education'. Underneath was a picture of Mrs Munroe in an orange high-visibility jacket and a hardhat. She was surrounded by men and the group looked up from an A3 plan. It was from her well-publicised visit to the building site for the new campus. Seven miles down the road, the girders had been laid. One or two of the main buildings were beginning to take shape. Munroe was slightly embarrassed by her fame. As she got up to chair the meeting, the fat man tapped the table to get my attention.

'I hope you've brought your hard hat.'

He turned to the grey-suited man beside him and repeated this statement. *I hope he's brought his hardhat.* The magazine circled the room. The three silver cranes involved in the new site's construction were now stapled on the city's southern skyline. Everyone was eagerly anticipating what Mrs Munroe would do next. She thanked everyone for coming.

'There are, of course, the usual hard workers here this week, soldiering on for the cause. We have some new faces also. I just want everyone to know they're welcome here. If you are with us for the first time, whilst a lot of work has been put in already, you've chosen the best week to arrive. We are at the forefront of the education revolution. As you've all been so kind to point out – I don't suit hardhats. But this magazine cover, exciting as it is, should not fool anyone.

'This is not an easy road. We might be gaining, finally, national recognition for thinking big about what this college is capable of, for taking a pioneering line on the kind of vocational work we can offer and the links we can provide to employers. But we are also at a crisis point. We have to look at what works, what is worth the money, and what doesn't. There are some sacrifices to be made. I want you all involved in decision making – at every level.'

She caught my eye more than once, and I felt a little of the fire in her, in me. Without realising it I had reached the end of my cup of coffee. The styrofoam still felt hot against my palm.

We all scanned the agendas that were handed around. At first I saw nothing of particular interest to me. Then I saw item number five – *Curriculum Review*. Someone slid the copy of *Future Ed* into my eyeline. Munroe's hardhat was a clean, pure white with rivets like snake's eyes. The Government Minister for Education stood alongside her. He had one hand gripping the edge of the plan they were supposed to be scrutinising. Behind them was the college sign with its new logo. A woman next to me asked if she could have a look. I hadn't got past the contents page.

I spent the meeting drawing several lines underneath item five. I went over the lines again and again, till the nib of my pen was blocked up with ink and paper. The pen went through the agenda and the resultant shred prompted everyone to turn and look at me. The secretary handed over a replacement copy. One of the governors explained that the builders had pushed the completion date back by three months. He pulled at his tie nervously and made a disparaging comment about their work rate. The estates manager laughed at this from one end of the table. He had drawn up a spare chair from the back of the room after coming in late.

'It was actually the original date, before Brendan was pressured into bringing it forward.'

'Can we look at item 5?' I asked.

'We haven't done 3 or 4 yet.'

'Brendan is yet to speak to me about this.'

'Item 5.'

'Will there be any more climate modules on the curriculum?' one governor asked, almost to himself.

'We might as well forget the agenda if no-one's going to stick to it,' a voice said from the back of the room.

Munroe brought her hand up and waved us all away. She placed it back on the table like a ceremonial sword as we looked silently on. She said it was probably best to skip to some of the later agenda items for now.

'I hope he brought his hard hat,' the fat governor murmured, glancing over at me.

'Let's look at the state of play with the curriculum review. We've got approval to run with the following courses: Floristry and Horticulture, Music – never in doubt, Law, Construction and – this is some breaking news – Counselling also.'

'What about the Humanities?' I said. There was a collective sigh.

'Well, apart from Law and Music, we're looking into a massive expansion of some Humanities subjects,' Munroe answered.

A conversation about class sizes and enrolment trends began to bounce around the table. I thought about my next class. I only had three students in it. Just then the female head of Humanities came into the room, apologised for being late and picked up the discussion points. I instinctively gave her my chair, trying to be polite, and ended up sitting further back from the table. Next to me was a silver-haired man checking his emails. I glanced over his shoulder then back to Munroe when he noticed.

'We're seriously looking into areas of the curriculum that

are low on funding and uptake, where we're not getting a val-
ue-for-money output. Those weak areas are likely to go, with
resources being redistributed elsewhere. We can move teachers
and materials to get a more rounded class size and an even
level of teaching quality.'

Munroe began listing the subjects under review. She
glanced up at me at one point, before calmly adding History
to the list. A member of the admin staff interrupted then and
passed Munroe a message. She continued almost instantly:
'Besides, it's not all bad news for Humanities – we're going to
offer opportunities for re-training in other areas.'

There was a murmur of consensus from the attendees.

'Like what?' I asked. My voice was a little shaky.

'We're expanding Sociology almost three-fold. There's
been a lot of success with a number of new modules. If you
think you're up to it you can be part of the revolution.'

Another teacher asked how long there would be before the
cessation of certain subjects.

Munroe smoothed her agenda out in front of her. 'It's a
two-year transitional period, so you can see your remaining students through to university or wherever they may be
heading.'

I was halfway down the corridor when Mrs Munroe called
after me. She had left the meeting on hiatus. She held *Future
Ed* magazine down by her waist.

'Matt, I'm sorry. I don't want you to take this personally.
Things have been moving at a pretty fast speed and I haven't
really had chance to sit down and talk it out with you – but
we will.'

'All right.' I sighed. 'I need to think about it a bit.'

'You're a good teacher. People like you here.' She smiled. 'Maybe I can sugar the pill a little.' She handed me a pamphlet. It was a flyer for a *Science in History* conference at the International Convention Centre. I scanned down the list of speakers and asked what she wanted me to do with it.

'I thought, as you had a relatively light schedule, you would be able to go along, get some inspiration, check out the competition. I expect you'll be wanting to give your own papers at some point.' She went to walk back up the hall then turned back. 'You've got a room at the Hilton, at our expense . . .'

'But I live twenty minutes away.'

'It's on our expenses, Matt. Don't worry about it.'

Then she grabbed my free hand with hers, letting my fingers fall open. She placed the spine of *Future Ed* against my palm and held it there until my hand closed around it. She leaned forward and I could smell the citrus from an orange she must have eaten that morning. Munroe was a bit of a health fanatic. A necklace of small pearls was caught in the collar of her shirt. She pushed the magazine into my chest.

'Give it some thought.'

I walked down a recently built relief corridor added to the main brick building. With all the facilities and resources that were based on the campus – shops, salons, saunas and even a greenhouse – it was easy to feel part of some modern utilitarian experiment. In some purely superficial manner we could sustain ourselves on site through whatever nature or war might throw at us. I came to the front entrance of the school for the second time, still clutching the Future Ed magazine.

As I approached a set of stairs I let one of my pupils, Julie, go ahead of me and she pulled her small black satchel tight to her back. We walked up those steps and I wouldn't have been surprised to turn back and see that each step had fallen away into some drifting mist. I tapped each desk as we entered the classroom. In front of me were three students. The pipeline that had got them here was already being dismantled in weekly meetings. I didn't tell them. I didn't want to de-value anything we were doing.

There was Julie, or Jules, with her atomic pink hair which came down in streaks over a layer already dyed cosmic blue. She had her lip pierced a little to the left, with a little blue stone in the ring. Whenever she was thinking she'd grip this stone between her fingers and lean forward in her usual oversized hoodie with her elbows taking root at the edge of the desk. She looked tense but I knew she got enjoyment out of learning. She was lightly cynical about everything and usually saw things the way they were. That's how she looked, cynical, as I asked her about the reasons for American involvement in Vietnam before '63. She swung forwards on her chair and I moved my textbook to the centre of the desk.

'Here's a clue,' David said. 'It's a game old people play.'

David shouted this hint from the back of the room, his usual spot. He was the brightest of the three, the third being Steven who sat next to Jules and was at that point scurrying a pencil around his notepad aimlessly. Unlike Jules, there was no telling what David might be kitted out in from one day to the next. For the time being he was wearing a crisp white shirt beneath a grey cardigan. He tipped back his chequered flat-cap and met my eyeline through the empty rims of his thick black glasses. He was a smart blend of Buddy Holly and Mos Def.

He had made me a copy of 'Black on Both Sides' after a few lessons and I'd listened to it two or three times.

David was clever but he was also impatient. I wasn't entirely sure why he was stuck in a middle-of-the-road college. If he wanted to do music, he could have enrolled somewhere with better facilities – there were two or three music colleges in the city centre. But we were lucky to have him, anyway.

'David, keep it quiet.' I said. 'I'll come to you next.'

He shrugged. 'I'm just trying to help her.'

He muttered this last bit whilst fiddling with some paper-clips. Jules ignored the interjection.

'Was it to contain the spread of communism? Ideological competition, wasn't it?'

'Yeah, you're almost there. I'm looking for a key idea. Eisenhower called it . . .'

She sat back. 'I don't know.'

'It's the Domino Theory. You need to get these key terms cemented in your brains. Eisenhower believed that if Vietnam fell Laos . . .'

'Cambodia.'

'Yes, and Thailand, would fall. The Americans were using similar principles elsewhere, in South America and Africa, but it was all to contain the spread of communism. So you want to get those key terms in. *Containment* and the *Domino Theory*. You can probably impress the examiners if you contextualise this sort of thinking in continued American foreign policy. In the years after Vietnam, the politicians lost their appetite for intervention. You can start drawing parallels then between Vietnam and Iraq. Be careful, though, they're not one and the same. Some of the reasons are similar.'

'Yep, like paranoia.' David raised his eyebrows and pushed up his glasses emphatically.

'It's best not to get sidetracked though. Iraq's a big thing. Give it a mention but don't start making unqualified statements.' I tried to settle the matter and move on.

'Why do you think we're there, sir?' Jules looked up at me. Her eyes were outlined with a thick line of eyeliner like dashes of newly laid tar. As she presented her question even Steven stopped doodling and paid attention to the topic.

'I'm sure David's got some strong opinions on this.'

'I do, sir, but I want to hear what you think. You are the teacher here.'

'I'm a history teacher,' I said. They looked at me nonplussed, blank even. I looked at each of them. 'I'm not going to enrich you with anything when it comes to politics.'

'It's history in the making,' Julie tried to argue.

Steven turned to her and offered his token input for the session. 'It's still pretty recent.'

'I agree. It is recent. Give it ten or twenty years and the truth might be a little clearer, once the smoke has cleared.'

David narrowed his eyes. 'Poor choice of words, sir.'

'I guess it is. You guys know what I mean though.'

They were still looking expectantly. Out of the window I could see the distant cranes, their thin fingers clawing at the ashy clouds on the horizon. I did not need to duck this discussion. In fact, I owed it to them. I walked down the aisle and sat on one of the desks amongst them.

'You know, if you're looking for reasons why we started this war, you need to be prepared to take on board so many different facets. I see so many reasons. Western governments want regional influence. Middle Eastern governments want regional stability. Some people in these governments think long and hard about how to get that. Some wave around their list of grievances. Some convince other people why something is necessary. Others convince themselves. Intelligence services want to find the information that supports the government's view, and always will find it, alongside a lot of other things they have to forget. It's never simple. It's always tragic. It always *seems* inevitable, although it never is.'

At that point I had an idea. I pulled an atlas from off one of the shelves. They needed to see history in a bigger context. I got them to stand up and gather around my desk. With a blue biro I started drawing a shape over the Middle East. I drew the shape of the fertile crescent. The line went around modern-day Turkey, Syria, Iran and Iraq and extended towards Israel and Jordan. When I had finished I stepped back.

Steven observed that it looked like a piece of shit. I explained to them some of the features of the nomadic lives of our ancestors. It was a lifestyle that changed when they stumbled on this fertile crescent of land. There was no benefit to constant wandering when they had a lush strip to cultivate, year after year. And so they became domesticated. Everything became domesticated with them, from their animals to the wheat and barley they ate. This was roughly 10,000 years BC. Cities emerged, the first civilisations developed along this strip, there was Jericho and Ur. The Sumerians blossomed. Languages, weaponry, defence systems, tools, calendars – they all developed along the fertile crescent. And the crowning achievement was Babylon, a name they all knew, of course, but none of them knew where Babylon sat, how it became the richest city in the world. I wanted them to think about how hard it was to equate that kind of success with the Iraq they see today.

'Our civilisation will fall too,' I said.

I remembered the exam papers I was meant to hand out. I watched them fold each paper and leave. David waved me off with his paper and left last, muttering some lines of a song in patois, of which I could only make out *Babylon*.

Only the giant map I had put up at St Edwards could have made that lesson any better. If I'd been able to sketch out the fertile crescent on something the size of a wall I think the point would have been better made. Whilst civilisation was established in the Middle East, our island was lost in the haze of Druidism. That was meant to be the further lesson – our own beginnings. The humble nature of them is best illustrated in just how small and insignificant an island we were for thousands of years. I could have pointed out that the size of the British Isles is always increased on our standard maps.

The classroom was empty. I thought back on the revelations of the morning meeting. I was on borrowed time as usual. My left sleeve fell down over the lesson plan I was signing off. I wrenched it back up my forearm and struggled to find a button to attach and keep it in place. There was a soft knock on the inside of my door, which was wide open. I looked up to see Kamal. The IT teacher's head shone with sweat. His tie was thrown over one shoulder. The other had a jacket resting on it. He looked around the room like he was staking it out and produced a packet of cigarettes from his jacket pocket.

'You free, squire?'

'No, I'm quitting.'

'What's that?'

'I'll be ready in a second. Just give me a second.'

We made our way out the front entrance where bikes were locked into the stalls and cars slid gently up the drive. We perched on some double railings. Often, we'd be mistaken for fellow students. At least that's what the kids who asked us for a light claimed after they passed Kamal his Zippo back. He would flick it shut with aplomb.

That day a small Staffordshire terrier was tied to the college sign. When a pair of legs passed close-by, the dog would feign some effort to sniff in that direction, stretching out his lead. I told Kamal about the axeing of my subject. He was concerned for me and my job and kept saying *Fucking boys' club* even though Munroe was hardly a squash-playing ball-breaker. She played tennis. I understood what he meant though. I expect he used the term to veil a sense of envy. It would have suited him to sit in the executive suite blowing cigar smoke into a wall full of mirrors.

'How do you join the boy's club?' I asked. 'It's too late for us, isn't it?'

'Afraid so.'

'Look at that dog. It's not right to leave them tied up all day.'

Kamal shielded his eyes from a burst of sunlight. We debated whether the dog might have been abandoned. If no-one claimed it we'd have to call the RSPCA. If they couldn't come out tonight then we'd have to take the dog home or put it in the gym. A couple, hand in hand, broke stride to circle round the dog, lean down and pet it.

'I'll check out here in a bit,' Kamal said.

As we walked past the gym, we slowed down to watch

the game of basketball in process. Frosted perspex meant we couldn't make anything out through the door but the shapes of the players. Their shadows flitted in and out of sight. The squeaks of heels turning quickly on the gym floor punctuated our walk. Another quick turn echoed through the hall.

A door slammed open at the end of the corridor and shook the wall. A figure was running at us. He got closer. We could see his white vest and his navy blue tracksuit bottoms. He got bigger and bigger, faster and faster. He was folding some money as he ran. He squashed it into his palm and looked up to see us. We filled the width of that thin corridor. He had a closely shaven head and ornate tattoos on his wrist.

I tried to stand my ground as he got near but he pushed me straight to the floor.

Kamal was shouting at him before he helped me back to my feet. My briefcase had fallen open and papers were spread around us.

'Jesus. What was that all about? I'll call security,' Kamal said. He watched me pick the papers up. 'Are you OK?'

I straightened my sleeves and looked down the hall.

'Man, I'd fuck that guy up if he comes back here,' Kamal said. He balled his fists.

'Yeah, I believe you,' I said.

He handed me a yellow slip of paper as I gathered up my case.

'Don't forget this.'

I could feel his eyes on me as I looked at the slip, a little confused by its reappearance.

'What is it?' he asked.

'It's this conference thing Munroe wanted me to go on.'

'That sounds cosy. Take the perks, friend, whilst you can.'
I nodded.

'What a dickhead,' he asserted, staring down the corridor. He strained his eyes and looked worried. 'That's not him coming back, is it?'

2

I BUMPED INTO MUNROE one quiet afternoon as she was grabbing her lunch in the canteen. It was exam period and the hall was almost empty. She told me about the latest remonstrations between the police and the college. A young man, who – Munroe was quick to stress – was repeating his first year, had gathered with his friends outside the toilet the week before. They were heckling the girls going in and out, first with wolf whistles, then with some lewd comments that were getting increasingly offensive. The guy in question deliberately threw his beanie hat on the floor as a girl wearing a short skirt came out of the toilet. Not only did he have a good look up her skirt as he picked up his hat but when her friend protested he groped her.

The girls – Munroe could barely conceal her pride at this – decided to get back at him together. Just inside the college entrance was the hair salon. I passed it every day. The salon was laid out in an L-shape. Through the glass doors three leather chairs were visible to passers-by. Most of the time girls would loiter around the corner by the sinks and out of immediate sight. There were wall-sized mirrors all around. They flirted with the guy, lured him in and sat him down in one of the chairs.

Just as he closed his eyes and started unzipping his jeans

he noticed two more girls around the corner. It would have seemed like there were more and more with all those mirrors around him. Several ranks of beauticians, each holding a hair-dryer aloft, moved in to surround him.

The four girls, a gang, although Munroe would not have used that word, started hitting the guy. One of them broke his nose with the butt of a hairdryer. Another burnt his forehead by blasting him on the highest setting. The guy tried to over-power them and ran for it. It was pretty messy by all accounts. She didn't know who notified the police but they appeared the day after. What pleased her was that the girls, following the assault, put in an application for new sets of hairdry-ers. She approved the application herself and fast-tracked it through the Finance Office. Police interest eventually tailed off and no-one had seen much of the guy since anyway. Munroe laughed it all off. 'You should have seen me. I was trying not to be proud of those girls.'

She was right. But I wondered what they would do if he came back.

'If he comes in here again – we'll get security to hand him over to the police for sexual assault anyway,' she added.

I passed those glass doors day after day. I saw legs swing-ing over the side of the seats. The girls were lazing around and chatting. They trimmed each other's fringes daily and placed each hairdryer or pair of scissors back on the wall-hooks when they were finally satisfied with what they saw.

3

When I arrived at the ICC for the first day of the conference I found there had been an amendment. Stapled inside each of the leaflets was a small slip with another name and title on. It was an underwhelming presentation and the alignment of the text was off in pretty much every leaflet. Clearly the speaker had missed a deadline for the printers, or else he had been brought in to shore-up a middleweight contest. His paper on Arthur Koestler would be the one just after the break for lunch.

I took the booklets back outside with me so I could smoke. I was early. Centenary Square was empty and seagulls perched on the support beams of the ferris wheel. I looked at my watch and walked around. By the registry office to the right there were statues and a homeless man was sitting at the foot of one of the plinths. I circled back around to some benches by a water fountain. I felt like the fountain was new.

I was thinking about this when I noticed a man across from me. He was taking long swigs from a plastic bottle and eyeing the theatre ahead of us with suspicion. A trilby was placed beside him. He glanced over his shoulder towards the wheel and put the hat back on. As he got up and plucked his briefcase from the floor he noticed me. Behind us the flow of the water sculpture lapsed briefly, before resuming and filling out the city's endless background noise.

'It's Coca Cola,' he said. He showed me the bottle of Coca Cola. 'I've got a taste for the stuff.'

I shrugged. I think I must have been staring at him without realising.

'I was away with the fairies,' I said.

He paused a second. 'You know, I read somewhere that if you hold Coca Cola up to the light the liquid looks red.' He agreed with himself, nodding a lot. 'Look at it with light shining through it and it's more red than anything else.'

He held it up to the cloudy sky.

'Not this stuff though.'

'Not enough light,' I said.

'It's not that. There's too much whiskey in it.'

He laughed. His creased cheeks and forehead smoothed out. He looked like a different person. He took another, longer swig from the bottle. I didn't know what to say.

'You know there used to be a sculpture here,' he said. 'It used to be where this fountain is now.'

'I was just thinking about that,' I said. I told him I could remember climbing all over the sculpture years ago with my friends. 'What happened to it?'

He said the sculpture was torched in broad daylight, on an April afternoon. The resin took light and the lurid, sandy shading of the figures turned black as a cigarette butt. All the figures, including Joseph Chamberlain, were mutilated beyond recognition. He said the artist had left Birmingham a long time ago.

'Well, no-one seems to miss it,' he said.

This man, in his suit with visible sweat patches, then wished me well and walked in the direction of the ICC. I looked at the fountain for a while. After a minute or two I followed him across the square and through the entrance. I was absorbed in the crisscrossing walkways overhead and only brought back to the ground floor by the arm of an attendant. There was a fine art exhibition in the gallery space that I had almost stumbled upon, only to be told it was by invitation only. When the purple-coated attendant saw my leaflet he pointed to a set of stairs and I mounted these.

At the top I saw the man from outside. He had hidden his Coca Cola bottle out of sight and was talking to a group of academics. They listened attentively. Their hands were clasped together behind their backs. When one of them was about to respond to his point, he turned to the side, saw someone or something and quickly excused himself. I sat at a table and waited for us to be let through to the auditorium.

I can't remember the other speakers; only Jaroslaw left an impression. That was the drinker's name. I got a good look at him under the stage lighting. He had dark hollows around each eye, indenting each cheek. His black beard had a sliver of grey at its centre. He was presenting on the works of Arthur Koestler. He began by talking about Koestler's suicide note. It had been amended over the course of two days, after his wife agreed to die with him. Jaroslaw delivered this fact with a grin.

The way Jaroslaw spoke suggested he and Koestler knew each other. He had the manner of a priest giving a sermon to unrepentant schoolkids. A lot of people in the auditorium were put off. A few turned in their seats and raised eyebrows at each other. Jaroslaw had a lot to say. He had a spiel about the history of science, arguing that there was a certain arrogance in the way the subject presented itself.

He said this arrogance was not becoming of a discipline that had produced the atomic bomb. He argued, and cited others who had held this same view, that science presented itself as almost complete every fifty years or so. This he put down to the perpetuation of scientific myth by those who were unwilling to chart science as history.

'The myth,' he said, 'assures us that, barring one final piece of the jigsaw, there is almost a complete picture of the universe and its workings.'

He compared the technological process of man to a TV soap opera, keeping our interest in an open-ended narrative that constantly deferred its own ending. All those philosophers who stubbornly put the earth in a pool or warmed it with heavenly fire, or who attributed the light of the stars to nails in the sky of the universe, as far off the mark as they were, Jaroslaw argued they had contributed. Valid ideas lay dormant for years and scientists schooled in mysticism made some stellar breakthroughs. At one point I became determined to speak to him afterwards. It was as he wrote off the generations of youngsters we were teaching, confining them to an intellectual cul-de-sac and rooting them in stale academic patterns.

I bumped into him coming out of the toilet. He tried to offer me a copy of his friend's book. As he held it up I could see the taught, freckled skin of his knuckles and the faded, pink outline of some bruising there. Eventually, I convinced him to sit down with me. It wasn't easy. I walked with him to the fountain outside where we had first spoken. 'Oh yes,' he said after a pause. We talked as office workers crossed Centenary

Square in front of us. A teenager asked if she could move his hat so she could sit down.

'Yes. As long as you put it on,' he said.

I watched as he tried to flirt with her, softening his voice and speaking with an affected clarity. She pulled a *Vogue*-style pose in the hat. It was probably the wrong kind of Madonna for Jaroslaw. He didn't complain. He put his hand on her bare shoulder. She lifted this off with a tut, turned back to her red-faced friend and put the hat down. He said, quite fondly, 'Oh, you are mean.' Before long the girls got up and left, heading towards the canal and leaving the bench empty. Jaroslaw turned back to me and asked again about my work, this time with a touch of venom, whilst one hand groped through his case to find the bottle.

Eventually I mentioned that I had gotten hold of Franz von Papen's diaries. I talked about the sanctimony of his self-defence in the book's opening. Whichever way history had characterised him, he had an axe to grind with his accuser. It was interesting to see the reputation that arose from the former Chancellor's choices. His was perhaps the best perspective. In many ways he had his finger over the button when it mattered.

We went for drinks that night, beginning on the canalside bars and adapting to each other's company pretty easily. We sat at a rococo table which rocked on the uneven paving. He became a little more diplomatic as he drank, supplementing his blonde beer with a toddy every half hour or so. It was a relief to see him relax a bit more, without reining in the precision and insight that came naturally to him.

He prised open my beliefs about the world, beliefs scattered and uneven until he had the generosity to start filling them out, broadening the spectrum. As we walked down by the canal I was feeling the drink and I confessed to him that if I couldn't take responsibility for the whole world, I couldn't take responsibility for the little things. I had brought up my feud with Wolfencrantz by then. He told me to forget about the self-made man. He turned his back to the canal and began pissing against a wall. We were on a fairly barren stretch between bars, one overlooked by luxury apartments.

'You forget about the self-made man,' he said, steadying himself against the brickwork. 'He's got nothing to offer you.'

4

THE FOLLOWING SATURDAY he phoned and offered to pick me up. He told me to dress as Franz von Papen. I searched my flat looking for a bow tie. I put on a grey suit jacket, shoved some papers into an old briefcase and looked in the mirror. I was just short of a moustache. My phone rang again and he told me we were going to a house party.

His taxi pulled up in the car park outside my flat. I got in and closed the door. I asked Jaroslaw if we could take a detour to the nearest fancy-dress shop. He was dressed as he had been days earlier, with the hat placed down on the backseat.

'Who are you?' I asked.

He shrugged. 'George Galloway. I always go as George Galloway. I'm running late so you're going to have to get someone to draw that moustache on for you.'

We drove down Pershore Road, south of Birmingham. After twenty minutes we left the suburbs and joined a Roman road. Jaroslaw said the road was haunted. There were often sightings of a chariot driver who had been out riding during heavy snowfall and ended up in the river. It was a small stream that ran alongside us. He pointed out the places where a car might slide in ice and crash into the bracken. We drove more slowly. I looked behind us for Romans. The rest of the journey took us down winding country lanes until we finally emerged in a small village. We pulled into a drive that was hidden by large fir trees.

There was a butler with a clipboard in the porch. Matthew Boulton, Imelda Marcos and Henry Ford had all arrived. Boris Yeltsin had been scribbled out. James Watt and Bertolucci were there. The butler found me on the second sheet, my name scrawled in pencil. He checked they had the right spelling. Galloway wasn't written down anywhere. I kept looking for it, lifting the sheets but soon realised Jaroslaw had already gone in.

I was handed a glass of Prosecco. It shook in my hand. A freckled girl in a lace bodice offered me black olives. She pushed one in her own mouth and turned away. I followed her trail across the room. There I could see down the main corridor and into the garden. Everyone was dressed up and I didn't know anyone. I tasted my drink and thought about talking to the East Asian girl to my left. There was no sign of my friend. I decided to guess at a few names. I started with the East Asian girl.

She was talking to someone about the influx of foreign players into the Premier League. It seemed that her companion didn't appreciate what he called an 'oversaturation' of the player market. Despite these reservations he was thinking about an invitation to join a consortium to buy Liverpool Football Club. Every member had to bring something to the table. During their first, tentative, meeting he produced a blood diamond from a fabric purse. When he heard the gasps of his friends he called them up on their objections.

'Don't you know why Liverpool flourished? You hypocrites! Millions of slaves passed through the docks!'

I realised he was Henry Ford but I couldn't guess the identity of the girl. There were bags under her eyes.

I recognised Matthew Boulton. James Watt was standing next to him. The latter was fretting and asking questions whilst looking at his watch.

'Where's the bathroom? When's the buffet opening?'

He put these questions to Boulton but his companion was already somewhere else, looking at a young girl sitting in a chair. He raised a glass of wine towards her. His view was blocked by the appearance of Erasmus Darwin, whose large figure pressed into both men and forced them to shuffle back towards the banister. Boulton said he needed to make a call and patted his pockets. His eyes came to rest on Erasmus' face. He said his phone was back at the office. With an air of vulnerability, he asked for his friend's phone so he could make the call. Erasmus sighed and said, 'Anything to further the cause.' Boulton stood halfway up the stairs and sheepishly made his call. Across the room we watched the girl answer.

Jaroslaw came downstairs with a bottle of single malt. He presented the label to me and asked if I wanted to get some tumblers. We headed to the kitchen. The East Asian girl with bags under her eyes stepped aside in the doorway. I felt Jaroslaw's hand on my shoulder as I followed his directions.

'Don't get sucked in. That's Madame Nhu.'

I went straight over to the sink to check the drying rack for glasses.

'Can you get me a glass of water?'

I grabbed a pint glass without turning around to see who

it was. I turned on the cold tap and nothing came out for a few seconds. Then there was a weak stream. I kept turning. I placed the glass in the sink and turned it again. The tap cover came off and the handle fell against the glass. Jaroslaw told me I'd misjudged the flow. Then water started pouring out of the valve, bubbling at first.

'There's a bit of a delay in the flow,' Jaroslaw said.

'Where's that water?'

'Oh fuck, he's broke it. He's done it again.'

A jet of water shot out and I put my hand over the valve. People were laughing behind me. I tried to direct the water down into the basin with my palm.

'We don't have Lech Walesa around, do we?' I said. There was laughter.

'Jaroslaw's Polish.'

'Yeah, but he's not a plumber.'

Cold water was spraying from my palm and I kept swapping hands. Jaroslaw was trying to protect Imelda Marcos from the spray. The crowd parted a little and a Pharaoh came marching through. Someone asked him to fix it before anyone told the owner of the house. The Pharaoh went straight to the cupboard beneath and tried to turn the water off. We walked away but Bertolucci, the film director, stopped us in the doorway. He wanted to get us in shot with the furore that was erupting inside.

Rather than fixing the leaking tap, the Pharaoh had somehow broken the pipe underneath the sink. Water was pouring out of the cupboard and onto the floor. We watched the Pharaoh slip underneath Imelda, trying to grab hold of her arm and stay on his feet. Bertolucci prodded us with his camera lens and told us to say something. I asked Jaroslaw whose house we were in.

My friend pointed to Lillie Langtry, who, in a tight bodice, was grabbing at some bottles on the kitchen counter. She stood thinking with a vodka bottle in one hand and washing-up liquid in the other. She began squeezing the cleaning fluid down into the sink until it was almost empty. Passing me the vodka bottle she bowed to the camera and started to dance whilst bubbles poured out from the cupboard and engulfed the sink. I swigged at the vodka, toasting my first ever foam party. Lillie was laughing, her cleavage shaking and sodden. We all began throwing the suds around the room. Bertolucci picked up a passing ginger cat and threw it into the suds. The cat scurried straight back out and ran into the living room.

Eventually someone overpowered the stream and fixed the pipe. Fortunately the good work had already been done – the ice was well and truly broken. I began to exaggerate my own character traits. I picked up what looked like an important set of documents from a dresser in one of the bedrooms and left them in the bathroom. I told Henry Ford to take charge of the music and, as he began tossing jazz records out of the open bay window, I leant towards James Watt to reassure him: 'We've got him under control, don't worry.' As the night went on, more and more of the guests greeted me with a nod and addressed me as 'Papen'.

Lillie Langtry tied her hair back and sat with me and Jaroslaw in the converted garage. She told us that she didn't mind how loud people were because the big fir trees surrounding the drive tended to soak up any noise. I asked what she did to get such a big house. Jaroslaw tried to give me a reprimand but she looked at me coyly, her blue eyes subdued in the lowlight of the garage. She answered, 'Well, Papen . . . sorry . . . *Franz* . . . I'm an actress. Surely you'd recognise me. I've just finished a tour of Cleopatra.' She winked and raised her hand. 'I guess you're impressed by all of this then.'

Jaroslaw excused himself whilst we talked.

Lillie waved him off and turned back to me. 'Did you finish the vodka?'

'I think I left it somewhere.'

'Jaroslaw told me you're a teacher.'

'I'm teaching at a college in the city. Unfortunately I'm on borrowed time.'

'Why?' she asked. 'It seems to me you'd make a good teacher.' She reinforced this compliment with a slight smile, touching the arm of my chair.

'Well,' I shrugged. 'They are axing my subject.'

'Can't you go somewhere else?'

'It'll be tough. My record hasn't been all that great.'

'It's tough to live things down,' she said and her eyes dropped to the floor. She began to fiddle with her bodice then. I couldn't tell whether she had gone back into character.

'I don't think I'm cut out for it. And I don't know what exactly I am cut out for.'

'Well, if you stick around with Jaroslaw he'll show you what you're capable of. He's a fighter, in every sense.'

'I'm going to get walked over again. It's like it's in my bones now,' I admitted.

She laughed in a way that seemed to wrap up the resignation in my voice, and put it to one side, like a piece of broken glass. 'Well, if you really think that's going to happen, what are you doing waiting? You've got nothing to lose. Change the dynamic. Make a move before someone makes theirs.'

'I can't do confrontation,' I said.

'You don't have to stick to the things Matt can do. Ask yourself what Franz can do.'

A breeze came under the garage door and shook the flames of the tealights. During our conversation one or two had gone out, a thin slither of smoke rising gently from their wicks. The front of Lillie's bodice was still darkened from the foam fight. She looked around the room as if there were other people in it. Voices sounded in the hall. I swirled my drink, thinking about what she had said.

'He can manoeuvre for power,' I said.

'Who's that?' she asked, trying to recover from some distraction.

'Franz.'

'Oh yes.' She sniffed over her shoulder. 'Can you smell that?'

'I'm not sure.'

'I think someone's smoking in there.' She stood up and stretched. 'I'll be back. Actually – you should have a look around the garden, I think you'll like it. I'll come out in a few minutes. The keys should be in the porch door.'

Lillie didn't find me anytime soon. I stepped out towards the looming shadows of those firs alone. There was a gentle wind. Everything was serene and secluded and I could hear the thin sounds of voices inside the house rise up and fall away again. I lay on the grass and thought about Lillie. Her generosity seemed impossible. I told myself to put aside the attention and whatever prospect it might or might not imply and to just enjoy myself. The firs rose over me, blurring together in the dark.

I looked up and into the house and I could see Madame Nhu with her hand wrapped around someone else's waist. A light went off a few floors above. I imagined the moon going off next, as if in sequence. I must have fallen asleep because my glass was lifted away from me. I heard someone snorting something, a raspy, panicked snorting. Shadows were standing around me and three figures came into focus. The Lunar Men had found me. As I sat up I saw Erasmus had the back of his hand to his face. He was staggering around, as if repulsed by something. Then he sneezed and knocked against James Watt. Watt steadied the doctor so he could talk.

'Franz,' he said, 'do you want any snuff?'

5

LATER THAT WEEKEND I got an email from Corinne. She said that Annabel was doing OK after the move down to London. There had been some problems with her initial tenancy but she had since settled. Settled where? There was nothing specific. Some of the email was an update about Corinne's baby, Micah. The rest amounted to a vague suggestion that Annabel, herself unable to contact me, wanted to meet up. Corinne added that she thought Annabel would be pissed off if she knew we'd been in contact. Nevertheless, she had mentioned me recently. It looked like my ex was concerned about how I was getting on.

By Monday I didn't feel up for work so I phoned in sick. I took a bus into the city and drifted towards Centenary Square. I slowed down for the cool air in Paradise Circus. The Hall of Memory was ahead of me, the ferris wheel beyond it. To avoid the crowds of the ICC and Broad Street I took a set of stairs down onto Summer Hill Road. Traffic rifled from the roundabout and out of the city centre. The architecture went from old civic-looking buildings to luxury apartments and then tapered off altogether. That was apart from two warehouses, spread out low and unassuming on the skyline.

I went into Wicks, the second warehouse. I bought a bottle of Lucozade and some yellow cloths. A little further out of the city, on the Ladywood Middleway, I found a phonebox. All the windows were missing. The cars passed in front of me as I leant against the top half of the empty frame. I phoned the police, speaking with two of the cloths wrapped around the receiver. I gazed up the road and saw a couple approaching with a pram. Their thin figures seemed to make slow progress under the endless clouds overhead.

The police called me back. 'Is that you?'

It was a different voice now, still female though, and she had some very direct questions. 'Where is it in the building specifically?'

I tried not to give her a hard time about the level of assumption in that statement. I hadn't said the bomb was in the building itself. After I explained this, and told them where to look, I hung up. I was unsure of my success. The couple were close to the phonebox now and I turned to walk away as the man called after me, wanting a favour, wanting money. I got on a bus and I didn't know exactly where it was going. We passed a hospital at some speed. There were lots of divots in the road and the back of the bus shook intermittently. Something in the engine was rattling all the way.

When I returned to work Munroe briefed me but it was Kamal who gave me the satisfying details. This is what I pieced together. At about 10.30am college security were told by the police that an anonymous bomb threat had been made. The device was planted somewhere on the campus. All evacuation measures were put into action and the students were directed out of the emergency exits by their teachers. Munroe herself made the decision to set off the fire alarm manually as many of the classrooms were not wired up to the tannoy system. The students were sheepish but mostly relieved. It was a lot worse for those taking their exams in the gym. They had been given enough time to fill about a third of their answer paper.

The Law tutor came in and told the hall that every student was to pack away personal items, turn over their papers and make their way to the back of the school via the car park. It was a struggle. Students between free periods loitered. Some were still entering the building. They were eager to learn but, eventually, security locked the front doors and got everyone out on the field.

The police called the school a few minutes later and spoke to Munroe directly. They informed her that the bomb had been planted at the back of the school, on a field, behind a fence and adjacent to a sign.

'The Bomb Assembly Point?' she gasped.

Things fell into disarray then. Five hundred or so students and teachers were lined up taking registers in front of this sign. Munroe tried to stay calm. She shouted over the crowd.

Some listened and began to pick up on the trace of panic in her voice. Other students drifted across the pitches. Arguments began amongst the teachers and students, and a few girls kept asking Munroe what was happening. She lost integrity quite quickly then, not even in being evasive but rather by stubbornly telling them to listen to her instructions. An exam student was sick on her friend's shoes as a voice rose up over the others. 'It's got to be a hoax. This is bullshit.'

Munroe grabbed the source's arm and then the collar of his shirt. Kamal and another teacher stepped in to restrain her. Kamal told me that by the time the police had arrived and the pitches were cleared, Munroe was sitting in her car with tears in her eyes. The police spoke to her there, out of sight of the students. Four hours later and streets were sectioned off around the back of the school. Bomb disposal units went in on both sides of the fence. On the near-side the operation took a few hours longer. The earlier stampede across the pitches had churned up some of the turf and the robot took time to gain traction. Kamal saw the police emerge with a crushed cardboard box and a Sainsbury's bag.

The units did not find any bombs in or around the school. The only destruction anyone witnessed was a cracked headlight on a Nissan Micra caused by a police van reversing in the crowded car park. Munroe confessed she felt like she'd lost control and gone overboard with the whole thing. I told her that was nonsense. It was a perfectly natural response, especially given recent threats, the current climate. When I used that phrase it was like something passed over her eyes. She fell into thought.

A day later I saw two workmen on the pitches. They were each in grey overalls and had lanyards dangling by their sides. Over the course of an hour they put barrier tape around the bottom third of the field. Within this strip the workmen dug a ditch around the Bomb Assembly Point. I sat down to mark some coursework. When I walked back over to the window, about half an hour later, the workmen were still on the field. The sign was gone and they were slowly filling the hole again.

6

A<small>T ABOUT</small> 4PM I went to see Munroe, expecting she might have left already. She was in her office though, answering emails and trying to sort out a purchase order she was making over the telephone. I told Munroe there was a Cold War exhibition that had recently opened in London. It was a chance for the students to consolidate their learning. She pointed out that they had already completed their exams. With an intake of breath, glancing every so often at her screen, she said that she appreciated the care and attention I was devoting to their overall learning but the money could not be spared in this instance. That was fine. I said I would fund it myself, so long as she allowed me to take them during college hours. It could, possibly, count as a bridge to their further learning, she said. She looked busy so I left her without really hammering out the details.

I went back to my flat that evening with some phone numbers I found in the student files. There were still stacks of boxes in my hallway. I dragged them in front of the television. For an hour and a half I filtered through letters, bills and paraphernalia that I had accumulated during my time in Sheffield. What I was looking for wasn't there. Halfway through a ream of letters that had been tucked back into their envelopes I decided to scan through some old emails. That was no good either. It occurred to me it had been written down, once, although I had never used it.

Discarded in the chest of drawers in the spare room I found a wallet I had stopped using a few months before. In it were lots of old train tickets and loyalty cards. Eventually, between splits in the fabric, I found a folded piece of paper. Corinne's address was written in thick black fountain pen ink. With her London flat as a centre point, I began planning the route and pre-booking all the tickets.

When I called Julie's house her dad answered. He said he would get her and then returned to the phone with an accusatory tone. 'Who is this?'

I said I was phoning from her college. Stairs creaked in the background. She had been asleep and sounded muddled when she took the receiver. Within a few minutes I'd convinced her we were taking a class trip and asked her to meet us at the station on Friday. When I called Steven his dad enthusiastically stated the house phone number. I thought I had rung up an office by mistake. Steven must have been standing next to him as I heard his voice immediately. Once Steven was on board I called David's house and it rang out for some time.

Eventually David himself answered. Without stopping to hear what I had to stay he started telling me about the exam. He was the most difficult to convince. His attitude was not dissimilar to Munroe's. We were done – what was there to be said? I told David that he made up a not-insignificant-third of my class and that the others were on-board for the trip. He said he'd come if I took them for a drink. Eager to get things settled, I agreed.

We met at Moor Street Station later that week. The rain had cleared and it was pretty warm that morning. The radio said it would only be getting hotter during the day. The renovated station felt like an annex of a theme park. Youngsters chewed gum in the cafe, their faces flecked by palm trees in every corner. When we mounted the stairs to get to our platform it was like trying to find the end of a rollercoaster queue. That appealing but musty smell of industrial fabrication woke me up to the day's possibilities. We could resurrect. We could make it up.

David had decided to go for a chalk blue T-shirt that day. Instead of a cardigan or a shirt, he had a long cord coat on. He began scanning the departure boards. A fresh tramline had been shaved into his hair. Julie was a little distant on the journey. She wrapped the sleeves of her hoody around her fists, making nervous eye contact. Both David and Julie listened to their mp3 players at the table. Over the course of the journey Steven would grab one of Julie's earphones, shove it into his own ear and start some exaggerated headbanging. She looked embarrassed every time. Otherwise, Steven was happy to ask me questions for the two and a half hours, trying to get some 'off the record' answers.

'Have you ever smoked marijuana, sir? . . . Have you ever heard of a strawberry surprise? . . . Do you know what a fleshlight is? . . . Do you believe in God? . . . How many arms do you think God would have? . . . On a scale of one to ten how hot was Madame Nhu?'

He seemed interested when I asked him questions in return. He was stumped on where the most militarised border in the world was. I left him thinking and throwing out answers for five minutes or so. Like a lot of my students, he thought of Israel's borders. Eventually I told him.

'The border between North and South Korea – the Americans still have a massive military presence there.'

He looked puzzled for a minute and then smiled inanely. 'Why didn't they insert their massive military presence into Madame Nhu?'

We wandered around Marylebone and found a fancy dress shop. David bought a Richard Nixon mask. He said it seemed appropriate. We got onto the Bakerloo Line and rode the tube until Lambeth North. This was about lunchtime so when we stopped to eat I revealed to the group that there might be a diversion.

'There's a flat not far from here', I said, 'where I think someone I know is living.'

I told them I needed help staking it out.

'I'm not sure we'll be welcome, but I'd appreciate it if you guys could stick around and keep everything on the straight and narrow.'

'Do you want us to go in or just wait outside?'

'Was this your girlfriend, sir?'

'Could have been his wife.'

'I know this sounds extreme,' I volunteered, and it was, but I wanted Annabel to see what I was capable of. These students were starting to show their potential and I had high hopes for their exam results.

'If you help me, afterwards we'll go for dinner, on the card and you can have drinks.'

You mean beer?' Steven asked.

'Yes. Just help me with this one thing.'

David was more switched on than the others. He slurped from a Slush Puppie and stood up at the table. 'I get it,' he said. 'You want to see whether she's with anyone else. I know what to look for.'

The apartment complex where Corinne lived was set back from a main road. Its car park was covered by shrubbery. In one of the visible windows over the treetops an exercise bike looked out over the neighbourhood. As I had thought, there was no public access. We had to buzz at the gate and then again at the door to the actual building. Corinne's thick accent came over the intercom. Our response had been prepared – David was to play the delivery boy in an Eastern European accent. Instead, I pushed him aside at the last minute.

'Corinne – it's me, Matt.'

She eventually realised which Matt I was, no doubt running through a weave of friends and exes quickly, in a panic, thinking that some skeleton had emerged from the underground to find her.

'What are you doing here?'

'I wanted to speak to you. I should have called ahead, I guess.'

There was a long pause.

'Who's that with you?'

'No-one . . .'

'Matt, I can look from the balcony if I need to.'

The intercom crackled as David shrugged. I beckoned for them to move closer to the wall.

'It's some of my students. We're on a trip in the area and I thought it was about time, you know, we spoke.'

There was some crying from the kid in the background. She went away from the buzzer and came back.

'I'm not letting you in here till I'm sure they are your students.'

'Fine,' I said.

The door buzzed and three of us stood back whilst David pulled it open.

'Is that your ex, sir? Where is she from?' he asked.

I told him it was my ex's best friend.

'What are you up to? Trying to get some nookie from her best friend?'

We mounted a set of stairs covered in powder blue carpeting and went to the second floor. Corinne was leant over the third-floor railing, ready for us. Her hair was curled and dripping wet from a recent wash. Somewhere amongst those wet tangles her mouth produced a barrage of questions.

'How many of you are there? Let them wait down there.'

I walked up a floor and came face to face with her. She had the door held open with the heel of a bare foot. The landing was just about level with the canopy of the trees outside. Moving to stand between me and her front door, she seemed much more diminutive than I remembered. This was the girl who had commanded so much attention all her young adult life, and here with her back to the door, she could barely maintain mine. I was eager to see into the flat beyond. The child's crying rose in volume again.

'Can you let me in?'

'Just you . . . they can wait.'

Seeing as I had prepared meticulously to get this far and dragged the students along with me, I hadn't put much thought into what I would say to Corinne. She reminded me of this fact when she came back with the baby in her arms and didn't offer me a seat but sat down herself, looking up with exaggerated expectancy after a few seconds. The living room itself did not give much away. There were two sofas at right angles, a television, a stack of magazines and one of those ubiquitous sculptures of the human form. *Cash in the Attic* was on.

'I sent you an email,' she said.

'I got it.'

'I don't remember inviting you down. Besides, Annabel isn't in.'

'So she does live here,' I said.

Corinne sighed and folded her arms.

'Is she happy?'

'I think you should ask her yourself.'

'Where's Seb?'

There was a knock at the door. Corinne went to answer it and David's well-styled head poked in.

'The security man wanted to know why we were loitering on the stairs. He said we'll have to leave.'

Corinne huffed and swung the door wide open.

'Come on in, all of you.' She watched them file into the room then closed the door. 'This leg of your trip isn't going to last much longer though.'

'Corinne, this is David, Julie and Steven. These students are all in my A2 class. I've got high hopes for them. David could get into any university in the country if he wanted.' She looked unimpressed so I turned to Steven.

'Hey, Steven, what's the most militarised border in the world?'

'Matt, this is not on. I'm going to speak to her,' Corinne said, setting the baby down.

She left us in the living room whilst she phoned Annabel. The baby played with the Nixon mask, cooing when David leaned towards him. On the other sofa Julie kept trying to catch my eye. I motioned for them all to come through into the hallway. We avoided the room Corinne was pacing around in and the abrasive sounds that were coming out of there. Her voice could be so unforgiving. We ducked in and out of the three or four rooms open to us.

Julie signalled that she had found the bedroom. She was right – it was undoubtedly Annabel's bedroom, although it looked barely lived in. There were two or three Art Nouveau posters on the wall. They caught more light than they had in her apartment. I gazed at the red-haired girl advertising absinthe. The necklaces on the dresser were recognisable also. The bed looked like it hadn't been slept in. David produced a photo from the mantelpiece. Annabel was stood with a guy on a pier somewhere. She was leant against the railing and laughing.

'It's the new boyfriend, sir. Looks like a dick.'

I shook my head. 'No, that's her brother. Keep looking. I don't think she stays here much then.'

I found myself shifting focus to look for the dresses and presents I had bought for her, to see if she still used them. Suddenly everyone's attention shifted to Jules in the corner. She was holding something up by a strap. The velcro crackled as it swung in front of us. She held it as if it asserted something more than itself. I thought at first she was being vulgar but saw that she was disgusted. She held it so far out from her body there was no danger the implement itself would swing back and touch her. It wasn't just a dildo, it was a strap-on dildo.

'She's kinky then,' David said.

She hadn't been sleeping in that bed but she must have been sleeping somewhere in the flat.

'Just put it back.'

We watched Jules dangle it over the drawer and slowly lower it till it made contact. The dildo's own weight made it fall backwards on itself. It extended over the lip of the drawer in a position which was untenable. She tried to close the drawer without touching it but the member's end became jammed. That was when Corinne threw the door open and imperiously held the phone above her head. She told us she had called the police and they were on the way. The students began to panic so I led them back to the living room. As we made an exit David offered Corinne the Nixon mask, adding that it was for the baby. She snatched it from his hand, crushing Nixon's features, and dashed it to the floor behind her.

Before she closed the door I tried to confront her. 'I know,' I said. She pretended not to hear, narrowed her eyes and said 'What's that?' then she threw the door closed and I heard her sliding the latch across.

As I descended the staircase I realised I was now alone. The others were huddled around a bench in the shade of an oak, still inside the gates of the complex. They were alert to the sound of the security door closing behind me. As I rubbed my temples I heard Jules tell David to pipe down.

'That is why you phone ahead,' I said, glancing back at the flats.

David was tying his lace. 'Is that where Nixon went wrong with Watergate?'

I liked his joke but it didn't seem to be for my benefit. We moped out onto the main road. Whilst I was debating which tube station to go to and where we could eat, David started to peel away. Within seconds he had limbered out into the road and was sprinting across a bridge, weaving in and out of groups of people, including some waiting tourists who may have got him in camera shot. He disappeared over the brow of the road.

Steven shrugged at Jules and began jogging after him. Even Jules, who had remained beside me, felt the pull of the flight. She looked back, her face screwed up in embarrassment.

'Sorry, sir, this . . .'

She shook her head and walked away, the slowest of them all. Awkwardly striding between people. Despite everything she was still insecure and uncertain of her steps. I started to follow but she turned back.

'We think it's best if we make our own way from here.'

Steven was gone by then, out of sight, with Jules behind him. It probably looked like Jules and I were having a domestic, exaggerating the drama by airing it in public. The passers-by formed a kind of moving circle around me. They were too reserved or uninterested to stop and stare. Outside Lambeth North tube station I bought a Coke and felt the shaking of my own hand as I tried to grip the cold can. I couldn't bring myself to open it. People were coming thick and fast around me again. I caught snippets of their conversations.

'I really want to go and see that,' a guy said, pointing to a billboard mounted on the opposite side of the road.

I walked towards the advertisement till I thought I'd be able to see the lineaments of Brad Pitt or Eric Bana's face. Those lines never appeared. A lorry let out a wrenching blast of horn as I narrowly skipped out of its way to the foot of the billboard. Without thinking I flung the Coke can up towards the board. It smacked against part of Eric Bana's beard, leaving a white tuft, a shred in the canvas. The Coke can itself bounced back onto the pavement. Some voices sounded in surprise and disbelief.

People diverted, first around me, then around the can which was hissing and spurting its syrup onto the kerb. As the flow lessened they began to move closer to the can again. As the last of its contents dribbled onto the warm paving, it was obscured by passing legs and figures until it disappeared. Eyes passed over me slowly. Even as people walked on, new faces in the crowd inherited their suspicion. They continued to look at me, disgusted, but without understanding why.

7

MUNROE WAS IN constant contact with me at the start of that summer, in an email stream that began with a discussion of exam results and kept going. I think she was purposely showing me undue attention. She knew I was one of a handful of colleagues who had not been a witness to her rare breakdown over the bomb threat. The emails she wrote were so affable. They smoothly alluded to the things I'd told her about myself. At the same time she told me about her own life as if she wasn't responsible for it. It was as if she wanted nothing to do with the conferences and meetings. I knew better than that.

That was the summer that Rafael Nadal beat Roger Federer to win Wimbledon. A lot of people said it was probably the greatest tennis match of all time. I didn't see it myself although I know it went on so long it began getting dark and they could barely track the movement of the ball on the court. It happened to be that day Munroe asked if I wanted to meet her for a drink. She managed to suggest perhaps the only bar on Broad Street that wasn't showing the match.

We were on the topic of some favourable results coming my way. It looked like my students would bring through a few As and be solid elsewhere. Steven was on course to get a C. Munroe asked me how the trip to the Cold War exhibition in

London had gone. We decided to order some food. I suggested we do more activities like that over the summer, to consolidate the students' learning, making sure we give them more than just exam papers to practise on. She nodded absently.

We kept ordering drinks whilst Munroe went through the college's board, governor by governor, and systematically destroyed each one. They were all chauvinistic pigs trying to pin her down as a control freak, or else they were neurotic housewives who couldn't escape the boredom of their own lives. I think she was trying to impress or at least appease me. As her eyes began to redden and fix on me with more and more drunken intent, she began letting things slip. Like the Minister for Education's hand had slipped onto her leg during their welcome dinner at his hotel. Such a self-obsessed flirt, she said, especially with the comments he made whilst she was strapping on the hard hat. She even managed to attack her own husband, somehow, through all of this. I wasn't sure how he had come into the conversation.

It was like she was goading me. I was the one man left in the world she had any respect for. And she asked me to go back with her to the house. It was after ten. Remembering that the Wimbledon final was on she said we could watch the highlights at hers. I went to the toilet before we left. When I came back Munroe was leant over the bar. Her coat hung from her shoulders. She was whispering to the barman. I stepped out into the entrance for a cigarette.

'I've got a feeling about Nadal,' she said, before we left.

In the taxi, she squeezed up right next to me and put my arm around the back of her shirt. I leant in to kiss her and her mouth was cold. Suddenly it was on my neck, her hand groping over my trouser leg. Whilst we were kissing, the taxi driver tutted. 'Take it easy, you two.'

In the house she didn't turn any lights on but we fumbled straight into what I thought was the kitchen. When her handbag got tangled around her arm she threw it down and the keys clattered inside. She was adamant about getting up on the kitchen counter and clasped one hand around the handle of a cupboard door. I was too eager to get my end away to take much exception to the abuse she gave me, which was the most consistent thing about that sex. She changed position every minute. Only when the counter had become a confusing set of angles did we go upstairs.

I saw briefly into what must have been the living room, a door slightly ajar and a TV that was left on. When I fell asleep it was to the distant voices of a chat show on repeat.

I woke up to what I thought was Munroe getting up. In fact she was throwing my clothes onto the landing whilst brushing her hair. I remember looking at the silver clock on the wall and realising it was only 3 or 4am. She saw me awake and stood by the edge of the bed, buttoning a white shirt that barely covered the dark line of her pubic hair.

'So I spoke to Julie about your little trip to the museum,' she said, turning away. 'You'll be getting a letter in the post. You know we hadn't even agreed a date for that. And don't get me started on whatever went on down there.'

She saw me put my head in my hands, disorientated, and continued. 'And me sucking your cock doesn't mean anything either. You don't have a future with the college. We have the staff to see out the rest of your students. There was a time I thought you'd make a valuable asset to the new college. You should have accepted my offer when it was there . . . Get your clothes on. You're not staying here. Your socks are on the landing and your shoes are downstairs.'

I couldn't believe her wild change of tack. 'You've got some problems. I've never been called a bastard so many times in my life.'

She rolled her eyes. 'Go.'

As I descended the stairs I heard her pacing overhead, throwing down different articles I had left behind. This stopped abruptly and I saw she was staring down.

'Do you know who won the tennis?' I shrugged, and she continued. 'It was Rafael Nadal.'

'Right, I guess it was.'

She leaned against the banister. 'They're saying it was one of the greatest tennis matches ever played.'

'It was his time.'

She nodded in agreement. 'It was. Close the door after you.'

I gathered my things in a pile at the foot of the stairs, fumbling through my wallet for any notes and preparing to call a taxi. Still half-dressed and, seeing as Munroe had gone, I gathered my pile and took it into the front room. The television was still on. In its half-light I could see the friction burns on my knees. I pulled my trousers on and sat down for a minute. When I phoned the taxi firm the guy hung up on me. I had no idea where she lived. Kamal might have said *It's a sharp left after the boys' club*. Somehow he was right.

8

I'VE BEEN THINKING *about those things we discussed. I can see they matter a lot to you so I thought I might put them into context, into this way of thinking we discussed. I know it's fairly new and maybe a little obtrusive to you but honestly, I think it might help.*

When it comes to those you see as being let down by the system – that may well be true but you need to see the system as an open-ended system of hierarchies. Hierarchies within hierarchies. They all give the impression of dependence when seen from above but equally of self-sufficiency when seen from below. This you might call the Holon. It bears two different faces. It works differently on the outside to inside.

The atom is not indivisible, although it was named on that assumption. The way you need to look at it is that neither are people, socially, I mean. We are not whole in any sense. The Hare Krishnas can undo that with one sentence. You might say that's a manipulation of semantics and you'd know better than me. Still it is worth thinking about.

Some of us are unable to function because the rules that govern us internally are different from the ones governing us socially, amongst friends, amongst peers, in crowds, in day-to-day interactions. That's not the problem itself. No the problem is some people can't switch, not without a lot of difficulty, between each set of rules. The rules are invariably different but the key is to recognise and live on account of the difference.

Everyone must be predisposed to their own rules but certain people have an unhealthy reliance on them. It may not necessarily be a bad thing, they are uncivilised by definition, but if the social rules crumble, if they fail, well those who don't rely are best placed to survive. There are those medical, biological examples . . . the cell that does its job perfectly as parts of the organ around it begin to fail.

The machine whined at the message's end. I took off my shirt and looked in the mirror at the small cuts to my back. They were little half-moons that had begun to scab almost immediately. The answer machine rolled on to the next message. It was left only three minutes later. Jaroslaw again. I angled my back in the light and saw some of the cuts were deeper, still bloody. His voice filled my flat again. He said he was going to Prague and Budapest over the next few weeks. He kept reassuring me not to worry about money and offered me his place.

If you could do me a favour – my house key is at the back of the hanging basket on the porch wall. Moses will need walking whilst I'm gone. She doesn't eat much anyhow but the food is in the basement. I'll be back in a week or so, I'll try and catch you in next time.

My flat was a mess. It was a dumping ground, a place to pick up fresh clothes or different ones at least. I could hear my neighbours below speaking in their low, cracked voices if I lay on the floor. The sound of cars came through the open window. Jaroslaw's place was not far from my flat, on the other side of Edgbaston, beyond the cricket ground.

I made late-night trips to walk Moses. I would cross

through Cannon Hill Park looking up towards the only visible lights. The moon appeared in and out of sparse clouds. Leaves moved gently across the lake. When I got to his road I saw paving slabs resting against the garden wall. I cradled the flower basket and the hanging roots as I untangled the keys.

My trainers were caked in clay. I left them behind in the porch and went inside to find the dog. Moses rose from a sofa cushion and shuffled into the hallway. The provision Jaroslaw had made for her food was brutish. He had filled an old ice cream tub with biscuits and left it on the kitchen floor. I decided to get some of the tins out of the basement and lay on something a little better. Moses ate slowly and with the kind of dignity I had never seen in a dog.

I wandered around the house looking for her lead. I had to go upstairs. Jaroslaw had placed a Francis Bacon picture where you might have expected a mirror on the wall of his bedroom, next to the door. There was a semi-dismantled television on the bed, half wrapped in a towel. His trip did appear to have been spontaneous. I hoped he was making inroads.

DISTANT SIRENS

I

JAROSLAW PHONED ME later about a particular meeting, adding that he couldn't himself attend. He asked me to go in his place. There was a trace of paranoia in his voice as he told me to stay on alert. They were his friends and had been nothing but welcoming to me, so I didn't have a clue what he was getting at. Still, I dressed up, in loose khakis and a shirt, heading out towards the south of the city on foot. I fell upon a retail park towards the end of my journey.

Couples were dressed up in their Sunday best and wandering outside both of the Italian American-themed restaurants. Sinatra's voice blew out the nearest door, along with the scent of calzone. A girl in a floral dress leaned on the menu-board whilst she adjusted the heel of her shoe. I was struck by an air of calm I hadn't found in a while. There was a notice in the window to my right. It asked for applicants for a position on the service desk as well as other menial, cleaning jobs. I looked in and could see a row of empty bowling lanes.

I went to take down the number but couldn't find a pen in my pocket. A couple were embracing now, and laughing between kisses. I asked them if they had anything to write with. She plucked a small betting shop pen from her handbag and told me to keep it, smiling a slightly crooked smile before grabbing her partner by the wrist. They walked off in the direction of a cashpoint. I wrote the mobile number on a piece of paper which trembled in a gust of wind. I felt raindrops on the back of my neck. I had to hurry. Not only was I late but, with the billowing clouds moving in overhead, it looked like I could get caught in a shower.

I found the house eventually. On the other side of the paper was an address for Juniper Grove. It was a neat sub-urban semi-detached house. There were children running around inside. Only cursory mentions were made of Jaroslaw and his movements through Europe. The children interrupted often and I saw no sign of Lillie Langtry from the party. I sat still, worried about spilling my coffee on any of the numerous cream throws that were laid over the arms of the sofas. Rain thumped against the bay windows as night set in. When the meeting was adjourned I was handed a rota sheet for school visits. As I was seen to the door I asked my host about the retail park I had walked through.

'Oh god, you walked here,' he said. 'Give me a second. I'll just grab my coat and get the car.'

His name was Dougie. He lived in the house with his wife, the diminutive red-head who had talked non-stop for an hour, and their two daughters. As he drove me home and told me how long he deliberated over his cooking for the meetings, I couldn't help but notice the car was a mess. It was full of bags and papers. When he saw me eyeing a satchel loaded with baby pink trainers he apologised with a slight stutter.

'It's f-ferrying these kids around,' he said. 'My wife keeps the house in check but they run riot in here.'

He told me the retail park had gone up about ten years ago. They had built it in the grounds of a derelict institution.

When it first opened, he said, he had been to the cinema a few times with his wife. Now they might go once a year for the bowling alley. It had turned into a hang-out for groups of teenagers now, the goths, the emos and the chavs floating around seven days a week, blowing a load of money at once then loitering outside and asking for fags. He seemed nervous when he spoke about this.

'Of course,' he said, 'being a teacher, you know all the lingo and whatnot.' He lifted his spectacles and placed them higher up his nose. 'Are you thinking of going bowling?'

'Actually I'm looking for a job.'

I directed Dougie past the cricket ground, to the turn-in to my block of flats. He stopped me as I opened the car door.

'You want another job? If you need more money we can get you more hours. We do the school stuff but we also do theatre work, open-air, museum days, re-enactments, anniversaries. Anything like that. It's a good programme we've got going. You don't want to get bogged down in something menial. Besides, Jaroslaw has got you covered, hasn't he?' He leaned back in his chair and stretched. 'What I'm trying to say is – don't worry about money. It's a shame if that stuff holds you back.'

I thanked Dougie for the lift home and said I'd see him at the next meeting.

'Hey, maybe I'll take the kids bowling and see you sooner,' he laughed.

I got the bowling alley job after an interview. They gave me three evening shifts a week and a discount card. I had to wear a purple polo shirt with black trousers and I was not allowed to smoke by the entrance. I dealt out the shoes.

A lot of the youngsters needed half-sizes and half-sizes were scarce. I was always chasing down the half-sizes, making sure they got returned. My superior was a bald, tetchy-looking man who discarded his energy drink cans in the bin behind the desk, rather than his own. I asked him more than once to re-order half-sizes. He would take another energy drink from the mini-fridge, crack it open and say, 'We'll review it.' Then he returned to his office where he sat and watched the UFC championships on one screen. The CCTV of the car park was on the other.

At least once a day, and despite my best efforts, the kids left after a game with their bowling shoes still on. Most re-alised when they put their feet up in the cinema next door that they had abandoned their trainers to me. I would line up the returned shoes at one end of the counter. The leather was stretched and faded in parts. The uniform brown colour of the shoes was interrupted only by the different shades of shoe laces. We replaced about three shoe laces every day. I tried to keep to white but often I didn't have the choice.

I did have an array of Febreze cans beneath the desk. I took great care to spray into the dank hole of every shoe until white foam bubbled from the fabric inside. Row by row I sprayed and returned them to the pigeonholes.

One Saturday evening I was re-lacing a size 12 that a six-foot ogre of a teenager had almost wrecked by tripping on the parquet floor. There was an obscure UFC title fight being beamed down on us from the screens surrounding the service desk. Christopher, the Polish cleaner, stood behind me and cheered for a Mexican in polyester shorts. The Mexican growled at the camera and tensed his abdomen.

I was explaining to Christopher, as he rested his elbow in a pigeonhole, that ultimate fighting was not 'wrestling for grown-ups', a comparison he and the manager had crudely made. I thought I was getting somewhere when a pair of black brogues landed on the desk. Chris tutted. I gazed into the perforations, the tidy grooves and the polished toe, into the reflections of our faces and the flashing screens. We breathed out. It made such a change from the endless display of Nike and Adidas. I was proud at the prospect of parading brogues on my shoe wall.

'Sir,' a voice said. 'You run an alley now?'

David was standing in front of the desk. He had larger glasses now, with thicker rims. He had a flat top, apart from the left side of his head which was completely shaven. His frames were still empty. Behind him were two of his friends, who hadn't taken their shoes off and debated doing it whilst we spoke. It took a few minutes for me to remember the last time I had seen him.

'No, I just work the desk.' I tapped his shoes. 'What are you up to this summer? Getting ready for university?'

He shook his head. 'I'm going to defer. I'm not going to travel or anything. I'm going to work and save some money.'

He was dressed as if he had just left the office. He had a thin black tie on and a grey cardigan. His friends were far more casual, looking younger for it.

'You don't fancy *finding yourself*?' I asked.

He shook his head.

'Fair enough,' I said, smiling. I was happy to see David so I turned to Christopher and introduced him.

'This is one of my best students. David knows more about the Bay of Pigs than JFK did. He's going places, believe me.'

Christopher shook David's hand then lifted his mop and bucket as if he was a standard bearer and headed for the gents' toilets. I gave David and his friends double the amount of games for their money. They made a fair bit of noise between them for the next few hours but most of the lanes were empty. David asked me to adjust the scores after it went down the gully. He thought I could turn things in his favour. It was out of my remit though. I went around the corner for a cigarette, soaking up the smells of the restaurants in the car park, and saw the three of them come out of the building. I called David over.

'You got your shoes back, didn't you?' I asked.

We talked again about how his year might shape up. He told me that he was taking history and philosophy for his degree, if he could get the double honours anywhere, and that everything was geared towards that. I finished my cigarette, lit another one, and offered one to him. He waved his hand and asked what had happened with my job at the college. I told him I'd had professional differences with Munroe.

A birthday party was going on at the Italian-American place. A bunch of balloons had been tied to the sign by a worker.

'What was going on with that woman?' he asked eventually.

Fortunately he knew when to leave it. He offered to give me advice on romance if I ever needed it.

A line of children were being led from a path to the front of the restaurant. At their head was a little girl with a paper crown. Whatever happened to children's parties at McDonald's, I thought. Then I quickly called David back. I could see his friends were getting exasperated but I'd suddenly had an idea.

'I've got a book I think you should read,' I told him, asking him to write an address down on a piece of paper. 'I'll post it to you. If you're going to go on to university then I can get it to you for freshers' week. It won't be on any reading lists.'

I went back in and relieved the other worker, Emma. After she offered to get us some coffees I pulled the bag of returned shoes from the corner and started separating out each pair, covering my face with a cloth when I needed to mask the rotten-bark smell of sweat and cheap leather. I lined them up on the counter as my manager approached, rubbing his bald head.

I sprayed the shoe, sending a cloud of white particles into the air around the desk. My manager had stopped to take in a pair of UFC fighters grappling on the screen. I watched the white particles form a cloud and then descend, falling onto his sleeve, briefly carpeting his hairy hand and dropping into his drinks can. Absentmindedly he brushed his arm. Then he stepped away.

The letter I had been promised by Munroe took several weeks to arrive. I picked it up amongst three or four others, saw the college's stamp and returned to the sofa with it in hand. The letter invited me, in fairly threatening tones, to attend a disciplinary hearing, with a view to dismissal if I didn't co-operate. I put it under the memoirs on my lap, open on the 'Night of the

Long Knives' chapter. One letter was from the bank, which I threw aside. There was another underneath, the front of which was bordered with ornate, golden strips.

This letter was an invite to Wolfencrantz's retirement party. The event had been referenced in my time at St Edwards. Apparently it had always been a year or two away. Yet the day most staff said would be placed eternally aside was in fact earmarked for the end of summer. I wouldn't have remembered myself and I had ruled out any hope of being restored to his confidence. Yet it gave me a lift as I put on the purple polo shirt and black trousers, combed my hair to one side and began the hour-long walk to work.

I approached my boss's office but found the door closed. Two or three people were standing around the meeting table with their arms folded. I was spotted through the blinds. A middle-aged lady with sunglasses on ushered me away. At the service desk Emma was giggling to herself.

'What's so funny?' I said.

'You,' she answered, with a slightly hoarse voice. 'Disrupting the big meeting.'

I walked around the back of the desk and grabbed one of the crisp packets she had stashed under there. Smoky Bacon. They were already open.

'Hey!' she said, snatching them back.

'Is it head office?' I said. 'He'll be taking some hairdryer treatment. It's only right.'

I began to tell her about some of the things I had seen in my tenure at the college. She said I was never a teacher. She didn't believe it for a second. Then she told me to take the reins from her, thirty minutes early. I agreed to, reluctantly at first.

The music began to get louder. Before anyone noticed me I emerged from the curtains and scanned the room. Bunting looped down from the ceiling. Some strips were the colours of the German flag and diagonal to these were strips with the Union Jack. There were no windows but impressive chandeliers hung from the ceiling. The quartet were on stage on one side of the hall.

A studious-looking man was asking his friend, over the rim of his glasses, what he saw for Europe. His friend replied, with his hand hovering over a plate of endives, that he thought the European Union might be a moral bulwark against US imperialism and unchecked Chinese growth. The questioner tittered at this. 'Moral bulwark? Come on. The game's up. We might be stronger together but that doesn't make us strong *enough*. We need to move away from Cold War thinking.'

They continued and he said that, on the whole, he thought England should be more like Canada. It didn't really answer the question. I moved between them and picked up a pork skewer. One of them told me that the plates were on the next table down. When I walked over there, I realised I was standing behind Mandy, the school receptionist. I grabbed her arm.

'Mandy, is Annabel here?'

She turned, unperturbed by my brevity, and pointed across the room. 'Why, yes. I believe she went to watch the band.'

I crossed the hall. At some point the carpet surrendered to wooden flooring. Presumably this was the dancefloor. There was a little girl offering her plate up to her mother who was busy on the phone. I put the remains of my skewer on the girl's plate and sidled through the crowd. No-one was dancing in the centre of the room but a little swaying and shaking had started amongst those watching the band. The boxers had just returned to the room and Wolfencrantz looked like he was preparing to make a speech. He stopped a passing waiter and pointed to the stage.

As a trumpet solo blared in my right ear, I saw Annabel watching silently. She was sitting behind the crowd on a set of steps rising up to an exit. Every now and again she was trying to see the performers through the crowd. For the most part she tapped her foot and fiddled with a crystal earring. I watched her give a little yawn as people crossed between us. Someone offered me a wine glass. I waved it away. Laughter sounded in the crowd. A strip of bunting had fallen on the double bass. The player draped it around his shoulders between notes. Annabel stood and walked up the stairs.

I went to follow but a hand squeezed my arm, pulling me back without letting go. Clapping filled the hall. Greg Cope was standing with several others. I assumed they were teachers also. He released my arm and started cramming cherry tomatoes into his mouth. I told him it was great to see him. Then I asked where the nearest toilet was. He picked some pork from his teeth. I could see Wolfencrantz conversing with a member of the quartet in the background. Greg wouldn't move.

'They invited *you*!' he said eventually. 'Well I hope there are no hard feelings or anything.'

'I'm not looking for trouble if that's what you're asking,' I said.

The other teachers were still smiling, looking between us and the empty corners of the room. They thought we were having friendly banter. Maybe we were. Greg began introducing me to them. My chances of catching Annabel before the speech seemed to be dissipating. I froze as Greg explained that I had quite the social conscience. He gave me a wink and continued in a low voice. He said I was ahead of my time in *that* department. Then he explained that this was a novel thing for a history teacher. One of the others leaned forward with interest.

'Oh, *you* used to teach in the satellite room.' She gestured to her friend. 'He used to teach in our room.'

I had been wondering who the wallflowers were.

'Yes,' Greg said, 'Miss Harris and Miss Killian teach sociology to the sixth formers in that room now. Maybe you could impart some of your wisdom about professionalism and boundaries . . .'

'Greg, I'm really sorry but I have to go.' I apologised to the others who nodded understandingly. I grabbed Greg's shoulder last, like we were pals. I told him to remember the ladies were here for a party. He went rigid and a tomato rolled from his plate to the floor. I moved off. The band had diffused into the crowd now. Wolfencrantz was tapping the microphone. Some of the guests gravitated in. A few families were amongst them. I pushed past and went up the stairs. The door was an emergency exit but it had been left ajar. I assumed that Annabel had gone out for a cigarette but I came to the foot of another set of stairs. There were three or four people loitering around. A kid ran down screaming like an air raid siren and headed back through the door, almost smashing into me.

'You came!'

Annabel was standing with a long-haired man who must have been in his early twenties. He was murmuring something in her ear as she descended the steps to kiss me on the cheek.

'I thought you would throw the invitation away,' she said, with a hint of sadness in her eyes, 'but you came.'

She hugged me again. Annabel explained that she had asked Mandy to send me out an invite. Mandy saw no reason to object. Apparently my dismissal was talked about in hushed tones between teachers in the corridors but it was of little interest to the reception staff. We hugged still. Her neck smelt of a familiar perfume. It was one I had bought her. Eventually I suggested we go up to the balcony for a cigarette. She said the stairs led up there and gave a modest wave to the long-haired man. He eyed us in disbelief.

The balcony was in fact a small pebble garden. A stream quietly bubbled behind us as we walked. Annabel pulled me towards the edge of the garden, looking for space amongst the smokers. Thick plumes from the cigars rose up into the cooling night air. We were on a precipice that extended out from the side of the hotel. It was amongst the tallest buildings in the city centre. I was giddy. Annabel struggled on the pebbles so she leant over and took off her high heels. She rested against me and I took in some of the fresh air.

'This is nice,' she said, looking around the garden.

I helped her to the far wall. Down below us a tram silently came to a stop. The streets were lively. Several queues lined the pavements, edging closer to the neon coves of each club entrance. Annabel squeezed my palm and asked for a lighter. I drew a quick breath and asked whether she had spoken to Corinne. I guessed that she had spoken to Corinne.

'What do you mean?' Her eyes searched my face.

'Well, she emailed me,' I said.

Annabel groaned. She wanted to know why. I began scrambling around in my head, trying to make something up. Then she dismissed the notion herself. 'I don't even know why I am asking,' she said. 'That's just the sort of thing Corinne does.'

I took a few seconds to consider what this meant. A bus heaved around the street corner, crossing the tramline. Annabel apologised and softened her voice. Her snap seemed to have been momentary. In fact she leant across and kissed me. Not quite on the lips but close. Then that sad look settled on her again. I said as little as possible.

'I don't know how much Corinne told you,' she began, 'but I moved out of her place two months ago. We had a lot of arguments. You can think the world of people at a certain distance and then . . .'

I nodded thoughtfully. Annabel looked out to the horizon where dark hills were meeting even darker clouds overhead. She didn't want to finish her sentence. All the bars and flats looked like they had slid in close to each other, down the sloping hills, to settle in the middle where we were standing, looking back out. She said people liked the view. She said it like she wasn't one of them. When I asked why she wasn't impressed herself she didn't answer but looked down to the pebbles under her bare feet. 'Did you ever have an idea of who you wanted to be . . . eventually?' she said. It seemed like an open question so I pushed the cigarette away from her body and kissed her.

Her arm relaxed and her tongue slid over mine. I felt the pangs of a teenager. There was that innate, soul-crushing loneliness that only Annabel could inspire in me. I clasped her hips and kept her close. When we pulled away I told her that I should have moved in with her when I had the chance. She was direction. She was as close to a map as anything was. I felt for the lines where I could fold her. I ran my hands back to the edges, where I might turn her around. She sighed and her free hand patted the lapels of my jacket.

'You are eager,' she said. 'I like it.'

She turned to look around the garden. It was likely we were missing Wolfencrantz's speech. I had heard him talk enough though. I looked around and there were only a select few still outside. Standing with his back to the city the man in the pork pie hat showed some interest in our conversation. He pulled the cigar from his mouth and raised it to me.

'Taking a break, are we?' He winked at Annabel.

Annabel shrugged at his comment and dismissed him as a weirdo. There was a pause for a few seconds. We strolled to another corner of the garden and I put my hands in my jacket pockets, feeling the cold. She said we had never talked about *it*. I thought she meant my departure. She meant us.

I shrugged. I told her that I had got a sense of the way things were. She didn't add anything to this herself so I asked what had been said at the school after I left. I wondered what stories had gone around. She said that, despite my ability to be an arsehole, the stories didn't sound like me. Maybe some bits got exaggerated and pulled out of context. That's only natural, I thought. As a counterpoint, she reassured me that I had always sounded worldly and it appealed to her. She wanted more of it.

'I'm not sure it's there,' I said.

'Why did you come tonight?' she said.

I didn't miss my chance this time. I told her I wanted her back. She laughed, shook her head and ran her hand over a nearby fern. I stood waiting for an answer. Not that there is an answer to that sort of statement. Still, why didn't she say something? Maybe I was floundering again. But I thought I had brought more conviction to the table than ever. Then I remembered how drunk Annabel was.

She threw her shoes to the floor and dug her feet into the pebbles. There was a clicking and scratching that sounded over her mumbled words. Looking up and down the black strips of the garden she knelt down. At first it looked as if she might be sick, but she didn't drop entirely. She pushed a strand of hair behind her ear. I heard her say, 'This one will do.' I didn't see the size of it but she stood up eagerly, leant back, and hurled a pebble off the balcony.

She looked back at me to make sure I had seen it.

'How many do you think I can throw until I hit something?' she said.

I grabbed her arm. She struggled and walked away.

'How many?' she said.

If I didn't give her a number, there was no telling what she might do. I walked to the edge and looked down. 'I don't think you'll hit anything that matters down there,' I said.

At this she pushed in front of me and looked down to the bustling street herself. I wrapped my arms around her waist. She didn't struggle free but turned into my chest. She kissed my neck and asked if she could come back to the hotel. It was nice to be an escape for her again. I felt her breath against my neck and pulled her in for another kiss.

The next morning I was sitting in the hotel restaurant. The expressway made a long drawn-out sigh in the background.

The high windows looking out seemed optimistic. Car roofs continually rose up and out of sight. My coffee had gone cold. A slew of different tourists appeared in the doorway, at regular intervals, distracting me from the newspaper. When I started to get worried, to doubt it all, Annabel appeared in my T-shirt. It was so baggy on her she had wrapped her hands up in the folds. She sat down with a smile and picked at the mesh through tears in a pair of tracksuit bottoms. A waitress came and offered us another pot of coffee. The waitress leaned between us to take the old one.

Annabel wasn't looking for things to go back to the way they were.

'I know,' I said, smiling.

2

Annabel waited with me whilst I checked out. We paused after the automatic doors. I was looking down towards the expressway. She told me where I had to walk to get the train. Then we kissed, sore and sleepy. I walked off in the direction of tram stops and library steps. I was in no rush. It was the same in the train carriage, gliding past fields. I laid a broadsheet out on the carriage table but couldn't take in any of the articles. The closer the train got to Birmingham, the more I thought about going to see Jaroslaw. I didn't want to talk about Annabel. I wanted to keep it a secret.

I phoned him and he steered the discussion straight to a living history workshop that we had been asked to give the following day. I didn't know about it. My work rota had already fallen by the wayside. We were due to be presenting ourselves as Roman Centurions to a year 6 class at Rubery Hill Primary School.

'You can sleep on my sofa,' he said. 'Then we can suit up and go together.'

I arrived in the evening and he showed me our costumes. He had not long picked them up. He asked about Wolfencrantz, got us both a brandy and offered me some watches he had bought from a market in Budapest. They were all in brown paper bags. Moses licked at the brandy on my hands.

'Thanks for looking after the bugger,' Jaroslaw said.

We woke up late the following day. There was an hour till we were due in school. The light through the window nets was stale. It had festered in the room long before I opened my eyes and glimpsed underneath the curtain. I was lying on the sofa with a pillow between my legs. As I mounted the stairs I could see Jaroslaw's thin shoulders hulked over the bathroom sink. He threw water over his face and looked down at me, the soapy water straining through his beard. He asked the time.

The shields were part-perspex and the body armour was crafted from tin. As I put on my legionnaire costume I began to feel weighed down. The helmet didn't quite fit and with too much movement would slide down the back of my head. Despite this the leather straps around my ankles and calves looked exemplary. I went to find Jaroslaw. He was busy combing the horse hair crest on a helmet. His costume seemed to fit him perfectly, with the swell of chainmail pulling in the wide girth of his stomach.

'Quite the officer,' I said.

'Thank you, and . . .' – he unsheathed my sword and tapped it on my right hip – 'yours goes here. I have mine sheathed on the left. If we're going to do this, we might as well do it properly.'

'Sure thing,' I said, adjusting my belt.

As I looked at my commanding officer I noticed something not quite right. Amongst the medallions attached to his chainmail there was a small silver coin. I leaned in closer to look at the face engraved into it. I didn't recognise the smile but there was some writing around it, a date and a name. It was something that belonged in a football annual. The proportions were all wrong.

'Why have you got Les Ferdinand attached to your armour plate?'

He pulled himself away. 'I was short a medallion. I had to get a work experience boy to improvise.' He hurried past me into the hallway. 'Come on, we've only got a few hours. We'll have to dive straight in. No time for food. The hunger will put you in mind of a march.'

We paid our fare and mounted our shields in the pushchair space. Jaroslaw sat his helmet on his lap and checked it for nicks or dents. I held onto the bars. When we connected at Five Ways and got onto our train, the carriages were brimful for a few stops either side of the university. Our armour pressed against the students around us. I thought I felt someone grab at my sword and my hand rushed to the hilt. There were a few grins behind me.

The wind whipped through the gaps in my armour on the wet platform. It was getting colder. The station was almost empty. We were on the edge of the city now. As we walked up onto the road the suburb unfolded on either side, in fits and starts, some streets proudly following the lines of the hills whilst others sank into the slump of estates. The prospect of rain was worrying. It could ruin our venture.

Using his shield as a windbreaker, Jaroslaw set up camp on a roadside bench and began flicking through an A-Z.

'This isn't right,' he said. 'I think we got off a stop early.'

I sighed and he closed the book.

'It's easily fixed. There'll be another train in fifteen minutes.'

'We're definitely going to be late,' I said.

'They won't care. They only care about the costumes.'

In the din of the station bridge we crossed towards the opposite platform. We needed to head even further out. As we began a jog, dragging our shields across the concrete, we caught the attention of a group of five or six teenagers who came from the other direction. The eyes of the nearest widened. He smiled to his friends and put up his hood the way Cantona might have lifted his collar. The way Kurt Angle lifts off his stars and stripes T-shirt. I thought about turning back.

'You got the time?' he said.

Looking back, that was an excellent set-up for a joke. *The time? Well, it's* 43AD. And maybe he was going for it. I could see little through my helmet but the freckles on his nose and a small cut below his right eye. He waited a long time for an answer from me. One of his mates down the corridor spat into the lift doors.

'I said *have you got the time*?'

Jaroslaw jumped in before I could muster a breath.

'Does it look like we have the time? We're in a fucking rush.'

Anticipating a reaction, Jaroslaw, the honourable and brave, then butted my aggressor out of the way, raised his shield and charged towards the rest of the group. I saw him struggling to unsheathe the sword. Everything unfolded then with a flurry of kicks and punches. I wasn't in a position to do much to save him. I was kicked in my side twice and then wrestled to the ground. The kicks were so hard I thought my ribs were cracked. I ended up in the lift doorway, further down the hall, holding my shield up against the kicks and stamping trainers. Our aggressors were joined by others, younger, who stood in the background and goaded me, curled up on the floor. Eventually I managed to fumble for my wallet and throw it out in front of them.

They checked for notes and cards, spat at me and left the corridor. I crawled into the lift and pressed the button with the hilt of my sword. It was bent out of shape but did the job. Before the doors closed, a hand slipped through and set off the sensor. The doors opened and I was joined in the piss-stained lift by two of the kids who had been watching the fight from a distance. I got to my feet.

'You got a phone on you?' one of them said.

The kid was kitted out fairly smartly. He was also indifferent to my struggle to hold myself up against the back wall of the lift.

'No,' I said.

I pressed the button again, trying to get to platform level. His aide quickly hit the doors open.

'Just let me get to my friend,' I said.

'He fell down the stairs,' he answered.

'I know,' I said.

They looked me up and down. They watched me panting and stepped back out of the lift. I almost thanked them as I pressed the button for the platform. I almost nodded graciously.

Jaroslaw had been held up by the sheer number of bodies around him for most of the fight. That was until his violent flailing had caught one of them on the jaw. They had backed off briefly, then came in again harder, hitting his head against the brickwork of the corridor. After that he was unable to hold his own. I think he had made a lunge for some railings.

The lift doors parted ahead of me. On the platform I could see a balding man with an SLR around his neck. He looked shocked and indecisive. A woman standing to my right was on her phone. She was calling the police. I asked her to call an ambulance.

Jaroslaw was lying on his front, bellied like a seal. One arm was bent underneath him at an unnatural angle. The shield had been left halfway up the stairs and had snapped in two. The straps around his calves remained undisturbed, and, looking at his legs you would have thought he might get up at any second. The toes jutting out from his sandals seemed to be bent towards the ground. The cruellest act was their removal of his helmet. Although it was next to him, I was later told it had probably been thrown down after he fell. All the head injuries were consistent with this. I picked it up and brushed off the dirt and dust in the plume of hair. I carried it for him in the ambulance.

Franz von Papen wanted to join the military from a very young age. His family came from a long line of salters. In his days as a Second Lieutenant in Düsseldorf, he liked to exercise the horses after a long night of partying. He didn't sleep much. His riding improved on visits to England. Looking back on his life Papen thought the hazards of the steeplechase were a worthy preparation for an exhaustive career in politics.

In June 1934, Papen gave a speech in Marburg as Vice-Chancellor. He criticised the direction of the government under Hitler. He voiced growing fears over the brutal tactics of the SA. Papen lost two of his closest friends and confidants, Edgar Julius Jung and Herbert von Bose, in the ensuing purges. They had helped him draft the Marburg speech.

Papen himself was held under house arrest.

Goering called after three days, seemingly oblivious, and asked why he hadn't appeared in Cabinet.

3

Mᴜ ꜰʀɪᴇɴᴅ ʟᴀʏ in a hospital bed for a long time from that day, on the wrong side of the survival instinct he had lauded to me in his messages. Maybe this was his way of making a point. They had to remove the chainmail with an orthopaedic cast cutter. A rushed nurse undid the straps of his boots and threw them into a bag. She asked if there was anything I wanted to keep but I only held onto the helmet. The doctor came in. After talking to the nurse he said that they'd better take a look at my eye. He did all sorts of exercises to check I wasn't concussed. He shone a light into my eyes but whatever he was looking for he couldn't see it. He shook his head. Then he said the nurse would put some Steri-Strips on my eyebrow.

I gave my statements, over and over, to the police. They said they would compare my account with some footage they had pulled off the CCTV. The doctor told me someone would ring the flat if anything happened to Jaroslaw. With that I walked out of the hospital. I trudged home, cutting across parks and backstreets to avoid being spotted by anyone. All my feelings had dried up after the third statement. All my words had been scrutinised. The officers had been just about to finish their shift. They talked to each other like I wasn't there.

At dusk, whilst I was walking, I heard a tapping sound. It was distant but had been carried on the wind to the path. The streetlights came on and lit the pavement ahead. The tapping sound would stop and then return. I was moving around the edge of an old industrial park, long abandoned. I told myself that the sound was some swinging beam, hitting a wall close to an aperture in one of the buildings. Or it was the overflow of rainwater onto a disconnected pipe system. It had a hollow ring. But the rain was nothing more than drizzle and the more I listened the more I heard a rhythm, lost in the swill of rain and wind, then briefly recovered, often interrupted by the sounds of buses on the main road and then finding its place again.

The rhythm was familiar but so out of context it took me a while to place it. It was more at home in the braggadocio of the football stadium, beat out in the claps of fans or blasted from car-horns during a tournament. Here, it was limp and distant. I found myself on the other side of the fence, via an unlocked gate. I walked between piles of brick, rubble and empty crates. I followed the drifting sounds.

The tapping echoed through a large warehouse that had lost its shutters. Its high walls enveloped me and sealed in the thick layers of dust on the concrete floor. Even as it darkened outside, the warehouse still let in enough light to reveal itself. I went through a small door and once again out into the rain. I thought I had taken a wrong turn as a flat expanse of waste, mudflats with large, crosscutting tyre prints, unfolded ahead. There was this boy, fast becoming a shadow, manoeuvring between the outcrops of debris, sinking into the mud then rising again.

When he was almost out of sight I started to run after him. As I got closer I could hear him. It was as if he was talking to someone and my presence was an interruption. I got closer and

I refrained from saying anything. He swore a lot. He started walking with more determination, looping around the piles of crates so he could beat out his rhythm. I was still dressed in parts of my legionnaire uniform. He came around the back of a hollow crate and stopped a few metres from me.

'Are you OK?' I said. 'This is no place to play.'

He spat some words down into the mud.

'Sorry, I didn't hear you,' I said.

I could see him clearly as he looked up. He had a face that might have been grinning but wasn't. In fact he was missing teeth on one side of his mouth. He had a hue of dirt on his cheeks that was spread thick over his hands. One of his hands was clasped around a wooden stick and, shy of tapping now he had company, he ran it across the wheel of a tyre in one of the piles. Around the back of the site there was some parkland and it wouldn't have surprised me if he was part of a gypsy family that had set up over there. He could have wandered through the gates like me, although not chasing any sounds, just his own boredom. The stick looked like the painted arm of a chair or a table.

'What are you looking at?' he said, and before I could answer he shouted, 'You fucking queer.'

'Don't talk like that,' I said, trying not to get angry.

'You look like a queer.'

'Fine,' I said. I raised my hands to try and call a truce. 'Where's your mom, or your dad? Do they know you're in here?'

He glanced to the far line of the horizon, beyond the fencing, as if he had no notion of being *in* anything. Containment was not this, the ragged line of fencing and the abandoned museum within the walls of the warehouse. Inside or outside might well have meant the same thing to him. He was like a bird that was half-heartedly attacking an empty seed-container, long after the cage door had been opened, long after he'd been expected to leave. It had been enough trouble for him to hear my voice the first few times. He continued walking now and neglected to answer my question. My right eye throbbed.

'What's that song?' I asked. 'The one from before?'

'I wasn't singing.'

I called after him, 'I know you weren't singing. What were you playing?'

Again he stung me with an insult. He was so blatantly free of self-consciousness that he might have been considered above it, were it not for that cruel streak of prejudice. The use of the word 'queer' was so malevolent and instinctual to him. What little his family had imparted on him for good didn't matter. They had managed to etch so distinctly onto his blank slate this sense of hatred. I looked at the boy walking through the churned mud of tyre tracks. I thought of the bigots that had raised him. I felt hot and my right eye throbbed faster. I lifted Jaroslaw's helmet over my shoulder and threw it at his hooded shape.

The helmet missed but the boy lost his footing and fell flat into the mud. I caught up quickly, retrieving it along the way. He struggled onto his back and I fixed my boot on part of his neck. It was hard to tell, as his legs kicked out and he scratched at my ankles, how much fight he really had. Was he clinging onto life because he wanted it or because someone was taking it away from him? He could have been driven by the same instinct that forces a kid to react when someone takes his chair or scribbles on his exercise book. His hands scrabbled at the brown, sodden leather of my ankles, briefly succeeding in ripping one of those straps away.

Spit bubbled out the side of his mouth and I watched him try to cuss again. He was trying to form the word that had come so easily only moments earlier. I lifted my foot up and snatched the stick, holding it in one hand and Jaroslaw's helmet in the other. Even as he got up to run he was not sure which direction to go in. He made the pivotal mistake of trying to cut back across me. He bit my hand. He was a vicious, obnoxious thing. Hatred in every pore. As one of his teeth broke the skin on the knuckle of my thumb, I smashed the helmet into his head and guided his limp body to the ground. I pushed him away so he wouldn't fall against me.

It seemed like he was still breathing. There were flickers of movement. His little finger twitched. I could hear air whistling through his nose. I threw the stick down and went back towards the warehouse.

All the streetlights had come on down the main road. It was fast getting dark amongst the piles of crates and the old car machinery. I caught my breath leaning against some boxes, looking back, hoping to see the boy scurry into the darkness again. After five minutes of quiet and stillness I began running. I ran through the open gate and across the road. All I could think was, he should have run.

4

IN THE HALLWAY the tiny neon blue lights of the modem lit up my shoes as I put them down. I didn't turn on the main light. Instead I could smell, as I walked through the narrow kitchen, the grease from pots and pans dispersing into the rooms. In the living room I was sure that over the outline of chairs and a small television there was a layer of smoke sitting at about head height. At first I thought the stoners downstairs had begun to permeate my room. But there was a full ashtray in the middle of my coffee table and I realised I had been smoking constantly myself. Whenever I came back home to try and sleep I forgot to open any windows.

I walked into every room and put them all on the latch. The curtains began billowing inwards. The red light on my landline flickered. New messages. I hit the button to listen. There was a hesitation. I stopped. It was the recognisable pause of an old man about to launch into a polemic about a chapter he had read. Jaroslaw's stuttering attempts at reason came back to me. I sat down on the arm of the chair and squeezed the sofa cushions. It was him. He was back.

Matt, I know you're there. I don't know how much longer I can put up with this. I was told you'd be all right. I've got mouths to feed. This just isn't worth my while. Not any more. If I don't hear from you in a week you'll hear from someone.

I don't like to do this to you, Matt, but for fuck's sake, you're not giving me a choice.

I rubbed my eyes. It was early. The hospital still hadn't called. I changed my clothes and pulled my waterproof jacket out from behind the sofa. The pack of Mayfair cigarettes on the coffee table was empty. I put on one of Jaroslaw's voice-mails and listened to him. I had to roll myself a ciggy from some very dried-out tobacco that was left over in a tin in one of the kitchen drawers. The tobacco gave me a headache. It was too dry.

I left my flat soon after. The corridor was quiet. The warm smell of marijuana lingered on the staircase, slowly rising to obscurity.

I crossed the park, going around the lake with the cricket ground's shadow fixed on the horizon. The housing changed after a few streets to Victorian terraces. After that it started getting sparser and shrubbery tended to hide the homes from the roadside. Soon I came to Jaroslaw's drive. I groped around in the hanging basket and untangled the keys from a plant stem.

Moses was ageing. I had taken her for walks but she had been hesitant about going through the canal tunnels. The Edgbaston tunnel took a good few minutes to pass through and was the longest I had seen on that stretch. Sometimes Moses would turn back. Once we had gone nearly halfway when she stopped. I had to put my foot on her haunch, pushing a little until she agreed to carry on. She dragged her back paws. We walked towards the light. The tunnel was too narrow for people to pass by each other.

That morning, I was almost discovered in the house. I was

down in the basement getting a tin of dog food. I heard foot-steps. It could have been the police. They seemed to stay in the living room. I could hear only one half of a conversation. When the talking stopped, doors were slammed. My hearing had sharpened in the quiet but not enough to hear what was being said. I stayed put. I turned out the light that was fixed to a beam by a single nail.

Moses paused at the door. I was crouched on the top step. She began sniffing my hair. She was confused and agitated by the continued absence of her master. I gave her a final pet and she watched me leave with her big black eyes reflecting moon-light. I clicked the door shut gently and moved away, crossing the unlaid drive.

I found a bench, checked it wasn't wet and lay down to sleep. I kept thinking about Lillie Langtry. I woke up with my hands between my thighs. My coat was lain over my shoulder. Foot-steps – heels, brogues – passed by me on the pavement. I sat up and a small crowd was walking past, heading out from Five Ways train station. I checked the time and got up. I walked to Centenary Square again. It was getting busier and busier.

I walked past the ICC. The ferris wheel had gone. The sea-gulls circled overhead. I drifted back towards Paradise Circus and thought about going to the library. I changed route and cut across a flowerbed to go into the Hall of Memory. I had to push the oversized door really hard at first but it soon gave. Straight ahead of me a book lay on a pulpit in the centre. It was quiet. I walked up some steps and looked down at the two open pages. There were names and dates carefully handwritten. Any commotion or noise from outside was obliterated by the hall's Portland stone.

After a few minutes of circling the pulpit and reading the names of churches and sects who had pledged wreaths, I eventually realised a door was open to the left of the entrance. It revealed a kitchenette. Sitting on a chair, with his head buried in his chest, was a security man. The high-visibility jacket was crumpled under his folded arms. He was soundless. His chest did not rise or fall. He was asleep but he looked dead. He looked as if he'd died whilst leaning down to hear the beating of his own heart.

Distracted, I elbowed a poppy wreath and sent it clattering into some bronze ornaments below. I closed my eyes, feeling my heart pounding. There it was. The sounds rang through the room. It was an echo chamber in there. Just as the ringing died down, a low cough replaced it.

'Are you trying to think of something to add?' the security man said, with his arms still folded. 'Add to the book, I mean. I can lend you a pen if you need it.'

I apologised for waking him and he pinched a white moustache thoughtfully. 'There's no need to apologise. I'm sorry I wasn't doing my job and keeping an eye on you. Has Naeem been in here? The other security guy . . .'

I shook my head. He looked at his watch, then produced a packet of cigarettes.

'If you'd excuse me, I think I'm due a fag break. I can leave you in here unsupervised, can't I?' I nodded and drew back from the steps to pick up the wreath whilst he continued, 'Thanks a bunch. Now – please don't set fire to anything or scratch a penis on the glass. It'd be on my head otherwise.'

After a pause and a haughty chuckle he added, 'The blame that is, not the dick.'

I called after him. I did have something to write down. I asked for some paper.

He went back into the kitchenette and said there were some prayer cards that they'd been given boxes of – for the schoolchildren. As they were going spare he passed one to me along with a biro and left me to my thoughts and the clear echoes of the hall. The card had a drawing of a dove on it. It held an olive branch in its bill. I opened the card up and, opposite the pre-printed prayer, a lamentation for the dead, I wrote my own message.

I added a name to all those kept in the hall that day, the name of a good friend of mine. There was someone else I wanted to add but I didn't know anything about him, not even his name. Instead I wrote a different kind of message. I called him the gypsy boy. The gypsy boy – I know you shouldn't say things like that. My hand shook as I placed the pen down.

Almost every day I was going to the Hall of Memory. I was walking from the flat and saving my change for the local newspaper. I'd sit on the benches and comb through every article, dissecting every inch of the columns. I was picking through it like the jackdaws picked through the discarded styrofoam boxes in the city gardens. Every death I found in print reassured me in its blandness: a car crash or a pub fight, a quiet death on the top floor, the surrender to illness.

When I would catch a word like 'discovery' in a headline I would panic. The same fear gripped me whenever I read of a teen reported missing. Fortunately the photographs were all recent and clear so I had no doubt that it wasn't him. I had just scanned through an article when the security man sat down next to me. He lit a cigarette and commented on the terrible state of the weather.

'Yeah, I guess it's bad,' I said and I closed the paper. Each time he came to sit with me I postponed my search.

He began to tell me about his old job which he had worked for about twelve years. He was toiling on the Rover production line. It was night shift work so he didn't see much of his kids, or his wife, but he came to enjoy the hours. He was soldering car doors or something. I didn't listen properly but he said he got to use his hands. That was until they dispensed with him after the first round of the factory troubles. Not the one that sent it under. He went quietly when there was no one looking.

'How do you feel about that?' I asked.

He tilted his head. 'Well, I have mixed feelings. I mean, my boss back then was a wanker. Plus, I ended up here and I like this job. I think you've seen why.' He grinned again. 'I can get all my sleep here and there's plenty of time for poker later in the day.'

'That's good to hear,' I said, hoping the conversation was winding down.

'Of course, I play it online,' he added.

5

I WENT TO THE nearest police station and pressed the intercom on the outer wall. It rang like a phone. I had been put through to an emergency call centre. They told me the station I was at wasn't in use and piped me through to another one. I was put on hold for a few minutes. When it finally went through I told them I had to report an assault. After several hesitations she agreed to send out a patrol car. When the officers arrived they radioed me in as a timewaster at first, seeing as I wasn't hurt.

I walked down from the station ramp and spoke to them on a mound of grass beside the building. It was about midday and a few people on their lunch breaks looked at me and the police, wondering what was going on. I sat down and ran my hand through the grass. A few cars turned off from the roundabout, passing us, and I saw a kid staring out, who should have been in school. In the interview room I had to tell them so many times what had happened.

'So you assaulted a young man, about fifteen or sixteen, skinny build, fair hair, blue or green eyes, missing teeth, grubby face, wielding a stick as a weapon, and this young man was involved in a prior attack on your friend?'

He had written it down all wrong. He was trying to look for causality that wasn't there. We kept going until he had all but blacked out the bigger picture. I asked for a drink and the other officer told me to wait outside. The hall was lined with noticeboards displaying maps and leaflets on civilian vigilance. The sergeant brought me a cup of water. She said they wanted to take me out to the site, so I could tell them again what happened and exactly where.

They made me stay in the car. My eyes settled on patches of dried dirt in the footwell. I looked up now and then to see what they were doing. Instead of pulling up alongside the warehouses, we were on the far side, by a fence and in view of the flat expanse where the body should have been. From there I had pointed out two piles of crates he had meandered through.

I watched the officers walk cautiously, checking the mud for any evidence. Occasionally they would stop and look at their shoes. The sergeant put an arm out to steady herself as she skipped down into a ditch. A third officer asked me questions in the squad car. All the same questions. Over and over. Finally he said, 'Are you sure you haven't done anything like this before?'

The two officers were trudging back towards the car. They took separate routes and one clambered through a hole in the fencing, further up.

'Maybe you didn't hit him as hard as you thought.'

I looked to the two outside.

The sergeant came close and answered her radio. When she finished she clicked the passenger door open and looked down at me. She asked if I had ever worked at the City College, not far up the road. When I said yes she explained that they were running background checks and had some concerns. She got back into the car and checked the mirrors. 'A Mrs Munroe seems pretty anxious to make a statement. Do you have any idea why?' She waited for me to answer. 'Well, it sounds like you're not going to be forthcoming about these allegations.' She turned the key in the ignition. 'I've got a feeling there might be a bit more substance to them.'

'What about the boy?' I asked.

'He turns up or he doesn't turn up. Either way, we've got some more questions for you.'

The door opened quietly and a concierge in white gloves beckoned me through.

There were several men, in military uniform, sat at an oval dining table. Over the large fireplace was a picture of Hindenburg. The picture and everything else in the room had a throbbing red light thrown over it. Hindenburg himself was sitting at the table with a serviette tucked loosely into his collar. He looked to the window where the red light burned from a distant street. A man with a moustache and a bow-tie turned towards me in his chair. It was Franz von Papen.

'What is it?' he said.

The concierge pushed me forward. 'Tell him.'

I leant down to speak in Franz's ear. He stopped cutting his potato and slammed the knife down.

'The Reichstag is on fire, Herr von Papen.'

Hindenburg started laughing. Suddenly all the club servants around the table joined him.

'Of course it isn't,' Franz scoffed.

I pointed to the window. The smoke was billowing out into

the night sky, lit red by the flames. Several columns at the entrance had begun to blacken. The shattering of windows and exchanges of shouting filled the room. The club servants began to panic. Two of them ran into each other and a plate hit the floor and smashed.

'That's fine,' Hindenburg said, standing up. He marched to the window, smashed it with his shoulder and threw his wine glass into the night. 'We'll put it out ourselves,' he said.

A beeping started faintly.

'That will be the fire alarm,' someone said, sniggering.

'Who left their phone on?'

My pocket vibrated. I put my tray down next to Papen. The ringing got louder and I pulled my phone out. I saw Annabel's name on the screen. I answered it as everyone around the table sighed.

'What's the fucking point?' Hindenburg said.

They began arguing about the likelihood of Hindenburg smashing the window. Annabel greeted me warmly. She was due to drive down from Sheffield in the next few days. I wanted to speed it up. Annabel asked about Jaroslaw. She wanted to meet him. I told her he was a busy guy with lots of commitments. It bought me some time. In fact, having Annabel out of the way had been a blessing in disguise. Now I was just looking forward to seeing her free of all this. I hung up on a good note.

I was trying not to think of the boy. The police had scant evidence against me and, of course, no victim. Munroe's statement had amounted to little more than suspicious and irresponsible behaviour during the exam period. She didn't see, or couldn't quite make, a connection with the bomb threat. It seemed like the dice had fallen in my favour. I guess it depends how you look at it. I placed the phone onto the table and gazed out of the window. I watched the Reichstag fire until one of the concierges went and turned off the projector. Papen put his arm around me and said, 'Great footage. How do you think it all went?'

At some of the seminal moments of German political life in the twentieth century, Franz seemed to be just about to sit down to dinner. Firstly there was his dinner with the Russian military attaché in August 1914, under the invitation of the American general, Funston. The two men were barely past the hotel lounge, let alone choosing an entrée, when Funston came bounding down the stairs. He told the two men Germany had declared war on Russia. The Russian Goleyevsky then politely refused to sit down. Papen protested, to little effect, that the pair 'had not personally declared war on each other'.

He would have worse meals, particularly whilst under arrest in the run-up to the Nuremberg trials. One Nuremburg meal saw another defendant, Schacht, throw coffee in an American photographer's face. Papen seemed to enjoy the solidarity of this incident. In the end he did throw in his lot with the others on trial. Though Papen would be acquitted, his reputation as schemer and fool remained intact, especially given his prolonged involvement with Hitler's Government. Ultimately, the thing that seemed to condemn Papen's fundamental guilt, if not a lawful one, was the fact he was still alive at the end. He had survived and people wanted to know why.

6

It was all greyed over outside and some small birds kept flitting past, on their way to the flat roof and back. I was picking up scattered newspapers and emptying the ashtrays. I found Franz's memoirs under the coffee table and put them to one side. I wanted the place to look pleasant when Annabel arrived. After all the pans had been left to soak I came back into the living room and deleted the voicemails from the phone. I gave each one a final listen.

Once the messages were gone I sat down. The carpet looked so nice I wanted to get down on it, to lie on it and do some sit-ups or maybe just lie there. I would have done but I was out of time. I put the memoirs on the kitchen counter so I would remember them. I would post them to David. He would understand. I pulled the window shut because rain was rattling against the back of the television. I prepared everything before I went to bed and I lay there, on top of the sheets, thinking of Annabel.

I was sellotaping the jiffy bag when she knocked on the door. She waltzed in, eagerly kissed me and stood grinning, looking around the flat. It was the tidiest it had been in weeks. Even the cushions on the sofa were plump and upright. When I went to fetch my duffel bag she found the parcel for David on the kitchen counter.

'Oh yeah,' I said, 'I need to stop off at a post office on the way.'

We drove to a line of shops bordering a triangle of bleached grass. An old man in a short-sleeved shirt sat on a bench staring into the middle-distance. The car crawled down the road and Annabel pointed out a newsagent's with a Post Office sign. She pulled up. I said I'd be a few minutes and kissed her twice, barely letting her catch a breath.

We had agreed that we were going to leave. We had ruled out all the places we already knew. It had to be off the map for us, which meant a kind of road trip and, with that, a kind of pact. I walked through the doorway of the newsagent's thinking of a dozen hotel rooms all at once, both of us wrapped in towels, Annabel uncorking a bottle of red wine.

I circled some shelves before finding the Post Office counter. The woman behind the screen asked me to put the package on the scales. I borrowed her pen to write David's name on it and I pulled a scrap of paper, with his address on, from my pocket.

'How long will it take to get there?' I said.

She gave me a number of options and charged me seven pounds sixty. The shop was fringed with St George bunting. It was match day. England had a European qualifier. The papers were making a lot of noise in the build-up. Eventually she called me back to give me a receipt.

I walked out the door and looked around. The last of the leaves were falling and they were being crunched under the wheels of passing cars. Two or three cafes were spread amongst the shops and they looked fairly busy. A man was walking down the road in an England shirt, in sunglasses.

A lorry drove past, on the same side as the England fan and, on seeing him, issued a volley of horn blasts. The lorry barrelled onwards, up towards a roundabout, and its hydraulic gasps started to fade. The rhythm of those blasts carried on, though, spreading through the streets. The old man even appeared to be tapping it out on the bench with the palm of his hand.

I was shaking. I turned and headed towards the Peugeot where I could see Annabel leaning across, pushing the passenger door open for me. The door swung out, then back a little.

'What's up with you?' Annabel said.

She kept apologising about the mess in her car. She'd had no chance to clean it.

'Matt, are you OK?'

'I'm all right. I'm just not feeling great.'

She said we'd go and get some petrol. And she asked me if I wanted aspirin or painkillers whilst she was in the shop. I watched her go in. I was rubbing my hand over the car seat fabric and trying not to think. I decided to make myself useful. I undid my seatbelt and opened the glovebox. I could do the map-reading whilst she drifted down country lanes. I pulled out some plastic bags and looked for the A-Z. There wasn't one in there but there were six mini shampoo bottles buried right at the back. I pulled one out so I had something to do with my hands.

I rolled it back and forth across my palm and clicked the glovebox shut. I looked at the label. It wasn't shampoo. At the bottom it said, 'Light Silky Lube'. I checked the others and they were the same. Light Silky Lube. There was also a paper bag of condoms. I looked up at Annabel. She was at the petrol station counter. I couldn't see her face for the reflected light in the glass.

There was something else. The car seat was too far back. She hadn't had time to tidy the car. I groped under the seat for the lever, felt the cold plastic and pulled it up. I moved forward about a foot before I was level with the driver's seat. Her mum was a big lady. Maybe she had been driving her around a lot. Maybe the lever was faulty. Maybe it always slid back.

Annabel was just getting her change and putting it in her purse. I closed the glovebox again, slipped a bottle of lube in my pocket and got out of the car. I got into the back seat. The car smelt musty and cool, nice and metallic. I lay down and stared into the footwell. When Annabel got in she didn't seem to notice me at first. She put a plastic bag down on the passenger seat. She put the keys in the ignition.

'What's up, Matt? Are you feeling sick?'

'You don't have a map,' I said.

'Oh,' she said.

'I looked all through the glovebox. It's not there.'

Annabel hesitated. She checked her mirrors and started the car.

'Always snooping around, Matt,' she said. 'So snoopy.'

She touched the wheel, was about to pull out, then stopped. I looked up at her profile. The bottle of lube rested on my thigh. She seemed expectant. I thought about asking: *Who? How recently? How many?* It didn't matter. Not now. There was something else. It was following me around, tapping a beat on thick rubber, swearing, laughing, spitting in tyre tracks. That's what I would ask her. She'd know. She knew that sort of thing.

'Do gypsies talk to the police?' I said.

'Do what?'

'Do they get on with them?'

'Probably not. But are we talking Romany or Irish?'

She said it was best not to lump them all together. That they probably wouldn't talk to the police. They'd resolve things internally.

'You're right,' I said. 'You're right.'

She started the car and we pulled out. We drove in silence at first. Eventually she asked why. I was surprised at how long she had taken. Like she didn't want to ask. Perhaps she already knew. Not in any mystical, clairvoyant way. And not like she'd seen it in the news. Maybe she had an outline in her head of what people were capable of. She sensed things about people that they would go on to corroborate. And long ago, she sensed this about me.

ALSO AVAILABLE FROM SALT

ELIZABETH BAINES
Too Many Magpies (978-1-84471-721-7)
The Birth Machine (978-1-907773-02-0)

LESLEY GLAISTER
Little Egypt (978-1-907773-72-3)

ALISON MOORE
The Lighthouse (978-1-907773-17-4)
The Pre-War House and Other Stories (978-1-907773-50-1)
He Wants (978-1-907773-81-5)

ALICE THOMPSON
Justine (978-1-78463-031-7)
The Falconer (978-1-78463-009-6)
The Existential Detective (978-1-78463-011-9)
Burnt Island (978-1-907773-48-8)

MEIKE ZIERVOGEL
Magda (978-1-907773-40-2)
Clara's Daughter (978-1-907773-79-2)